THE BIG
GOLD DREAM

Other titles in the Allison & Busby American Crime Series

THE BIG GOLD DREAM

Chester Himes

Allison & Busby
Published by W.H. Allen & Co. Plc

An Allison & Busby book
Published in 1988 by
W.H. Allen & Co. Plc
44 Hill Street
London WIX 8LB

Typeset by AKM Associates (UK) Ltd,
Ajmal House, Hayes Road, Southall, London
Printed and bound in Great Britain by
Anchor Brendon Ltd., Tiptree, Essex

ISBN 0 85031 891 2

1

"Faith is a rock! It's like a solid gold dream!"

The voice of the Sweet Prophet Brown issued from the amplifiers atop a sound truck and reverberated from the shabby brick faces of the tenement houses flanking 117th Street

"Amen!" Alberta Wright said fervently.

Her big brown cowlike eyes cast a look of adoration across the gleaming white sea of kneeling worshipers upon Sweet Prophet's exalted black face. She felt as though he were addressing her personally, although she was only one of six hundred white-robed converts kneeling in the noonday sun on the burning hot asphalt.

"On this dream every church in all the world is built," Sweet Prophet continued lyrically.

A moaning fervor passed over the kneeling figures like a cool breeze. Spectators and converts alike were gripped, in dead seriousness, as though cast under a spell.

Black, brown and yellow people packed the sidewalks all the way from Seventh Avenue to Lenox Avenue. They crowded into the tenement windows, jammed the smelly doorways, clung to the sides of electric light poles and stood on garbage cans to watch the performance of this fabulous man.

Sweating foot cops in wet clinging shirts and mounted cops on lathered horses surrounded Sweet Prophet's throne to keep back the mob. The street had been closed off at both ends by a police barrier. Sweet Prophet sat on a throne of red roses on a flower-draped float at one end of the block and spoke into a microphone connected to a sound truck behind him. Over his head was a sunshade of gold tinsel made in the shape of a halo. About his feet was a circle of little black girls dressed as angels.

He threw back his head and said, in a voice of indubitable sincerity, "Faith is so powerful it will turn this dirty black pavement into gleaming gold."

"Don't I know it!" Alberta said aloud.

Her hand closed about Sugar Stonewall's fingers like a steel vice. Dressed in a wrinkled rayon sports ensemble, he knelt on the pavement beside her. She had insisted that he be near her in this great hour of triumph, even though he had not been converted. But she did not look at him; her eyes were closed. Tears trickled down her smooth brown skin.

"Put your trust in The Lord," Sweet Prophet said.

Suddenly Alberta was on her feet. "I did!" she cried, arms upraised. "I did! I put my trust in Him and He sent me a dream because I had faith."

"Kneel down, honey," Sugar pleaded. "You're messing up the service."

But his plea went unheeded. Alberta was a big, muscular woman with a flat, pretty face, now contorted in ecstasy. Clad in a tight-fitting white maid's uniform, her long-fingered hands reaching toward the sky, she drew everyone's attention. Her ecstasy was contagious.

"Amen!" the converts chorused.

With the natural-born instinct of a master showman, Sweet Prophet sensed the sympathetic mood. He interrupted his dissertation and said, "Tell us your dream, sister."

"I dreamed I was baking three apple pies," she said. "And when I took them out the oven and set them on the table to cool the crusts busted open like three explosions and the whole kitchen was filled with hundred dollar bills."

"My God!" a worshiper exclaimed.

"Money!" another cried.

"Money! Money! Money!" others chorused.

Even Sweet Prophet looked impressed. "And did you have faith, sister?" he asked.

"I had faith!" Alberta declared.

"Hush up, honey, for Christ's sake," Sugar Stonewall warned.

But she paid him no attention. "I had faith!" she repeated. "And God didn't fail me. God has set me free."

"Amen!" the worshipers chorused with heartfelt earnestness.

Upon this note Sweet Prophet stood and raised his hands for silence. His tremendous bulk was impressive in a bright purple robe lined with yellow silk and trimmed with mink. Beneath it he wore a black taffeta suit with white piping and silver buttons. His fingernails, untrimmed since he first claimed to have spoken with God, were more than three inches in length. They curled like strange talons, and were painted different colors. On each finger he wore a diamond ring. His smooth black face with its big buck teeth and popping eyes was ageless; but his long grizzly hair, on which he

6

wore a black silk cap, was snow-white.

Silence descended over the multitude like night.

"I now baptize you, who have seen the glory and harkened to the call, in the name of the Father, the Son and the Holy Ghost," he said.

Sugar Stonewall picked up the basket of lunch Alberta had prepared for the celebration afterward and beat it for the sidelines. And not a moment too soon.

At the completion of Sweet Prophet's words, fire hoses at each end of the block manned by stalwart deacons, were turned on simultaneously. Stream of water shot high into the air and came down upon white-clad figures in a veritable deluge.

Drenched by the cold holy water pouring from heaven, the converts, most of whom were women, were seized by uncontrollable ecstasy. They danced and screamed and shouted and moaned, carried away with emotion, caught up in a mass delirium. They sang and prayed, gasped and strangled in a frenzy of exultation.

A buxom woman cried, "My skin may be black, but my soul ain't got no color."

"Wash me as white as snow," another screamed, tearing off her dress so that the purifying water could wash her naked skin.

"I had faith, didn't I, God?" Alberta chanted, caught up in the mass hysteria, her transfigured face turned toward heaven. Water flowed unnoticed into her nostrils, almost strangling her. "I had faith!" she continued, sputtering. "And you didn't fail me God."

Finally the hoses were turned off, and Sweet Prophet's church band, arranged about the sound truck, began to play hymns in rock and roll time.

The drenched, half-drowned converts crowded about the throne of Sweet Prophet to buy bread crumbs, which he took from the pockets of his robe. They paid from one to twenty dollars per crumb.

Waving the sheafs of greenbacks he held between his long twisted varicolored fingernails, he crooned ardently, "Faith will reduce the Pacific Ocean to a drop of water; it will change the Rocky Mountains into a grain of sand."

Other persons from among the multitudes of spectators had come to have their infirmities cured by the touch of Sweet Prophet's hand. Hands lifted a cripped child. A paralysed woman was wheeled forward on a stretcher. A worried-looking man extended an eviction notice. Numbers slips for that day's play were

7

brushed against the throne; a pair of dice were surreptitiously rubbed against the hem of Sweet Prophet's robe.

Alberta Wright found Sugar Stonewall sitting in a crowded doorway. He gave her the bottle of drinking water from the lunch basket and told her to go and have the prophet bless it.

She fought her way to the side of the float and held the bottle aloft. Sweet Prophet recognized her, and a look passed between them. He reached forth a long-nailed hand and touched the lip of the bottle.

"Out of this water will come miracles," he intoned.

"Amen," a woman said.

Alberta looked dazed. As though stunned by the magnitude of her good fortune, she dug a wet $50 bill from her brassiere and thrust it toward Sweet Prophet. In return she received a bread crumb the size of a garden pea. She put the crumb into her mouth, looking heavenward, and washed it down with water from the blessed bottle, drinking long and heartily.

Everyone who looked on the scene was convinced the water had been imbued with healing powers.

Suddenly Alberta began to leap and dance in a frenzy of exultation. Her big-boned body shook like a nautch dancer. Her face shone with religious fervor.

"I got Him inside of me!" she cried. "I got God inside of me. I can feel Him inside of my stomach."

The spectators were caught between amusement and awe.

"I can feel Him in my bones!" Alberta screamed. "He's in my blood."

She was shaking in a very delirium of passion.

"Oh, where is my Sugar?" she cried. "Sugar Stonewall!" she called. "Where are you, Sugar?"

Suddenly the faces blurred in her vision. The sky took on the colors of the spectrum, as though the world had turned into a rainbow. Her eyes protruded from her head, and sweat beaded all over her face. She began to moan and whimper, as though the ecstasy was more than she could bear; then she staggered and reeled, fell on to the street and lay twitching on the wet pavement, from which steam had begun to rise.

"She's having a fit," someone cried.

The crowd surged forward. Faces were distorted with excitement. People struggled frantically to get a look.

Sweet Prophet realized something unusual was happening. With quick presence of mind, he signaled his band to begin playing *When*

The Saints Come Marching In, then beckoned to his top elder, Reverend Jones.

Elder Jones was on the alert, as always. Dressed in a gold-braided white uniform with colored tassels sprouting from the shoulders, like a rear admiral in the Cuban navy, he ascended the dais and bent toward the throne, cupping a hand to his ear.

"See what is happening to that woman down there," Sweet Prophet directed.

Elder Jones descended to the street and knelt beside Alberta. His expression became grave. The spectators hemmed him in, leaning over his shoulders, and bombarded him with questions.

"Get back," he ordered sharply. "Give the sister air. She's had a trance. She's gone to talk with God."

The spectators backed away with awed expressions. But still he had to conduct his examination with the utmost circumspection. He held Alberta's hand while furtively seeking her pulse – he didn't find any. He looked at her nostrils, and there was no movement. Her eyes had rolled back into her head so that only the whites showed. He stroked her face, feeling for the vein in the temple, but her skin was like cooling wax. He would have liked to put a mirror over her mouth, but couldn't risk alarming the spectators. He was so terrified he could hardly breathe, but he kept repeating, "Glory be to Jesus," to camouflage his fears. He requested the police to keep back the crowd, then climbed slowly to the throne dais.

Sweet Prophet gave one look at Elder Jones' black face, which had dried to the texture of wood ashes, and expected the worst. "Well?" he asked fearfully.

"She looks dead to me," Elder Jones reported.

Sweet Prophet's already protruding eyes bulged perilously from their sockets. "Great God Almighty!" he whispered in a tone of consternation. "How in God's name could that happen?"

Elder Jones' mouth felt cotton-dry, and the hot air burned inside of his nostrils. "The only way I figure it could have happened is the water you blessed was poisoned," he said.

"Lord in Heaven help us," Sweet Prophet moaned. "How could it be poisoned?"

"Only God knows," Elder Jones said.

Sweet Prophet drew a bottle of smelling salts from somewhere beneath his robe and held it to his nose. He couldn't afford to faint in this emergency, but his head whirled in a blind panic.

He pulled a yellow silk handkerchief from his pocket and patted his forehead.

"Are you certain she's dead, Elder?" he asked with a faint remnant of hope.

"I couldn't find any pulse, and she sure looks dead," the other affirmed.

As luck would have it, one of the little angels encircling the prophet's throne overheard the elder. Her eyes stretched, and her mouth dropped open.

"Daid? Is she really and truly daid?"

"Hush, child," Sweet Prophet said anxiously, but it was too late.

A spectator had heard her – a big bull-voiced man wearing purple suspenders over a yellow shirt.

"Great jumping Jehoshaphat, she ain't in no trance!" he shouted in a voice that carried above the marching brass of the band. "She is plumb dead!"

"Shut up, fool!" Elder Jones shouted. "Do you want to panic everybody?"

But the damage was done. Word ran through the crowd like quicksilver that the converted woman who had drunk of the holy water had dropped dead.

Pandemonium broke loose. Emotions already ignited by religious fervor skyrocketed in terror. The excitable people began milling and screaming and fighting one another in animal panic.

Sweet Prophet knew he had to do something quick to avert catastrophe. It was the most desperate situation he had ever faced in his long and checkered career as a revivalist. It was worse even than the time he had been accused of raping three twelve-year-old girls.

His whole career hung in the balance. The next twenty minutes would determine the fate of his cult, which had taken him twenty years to build up. Not only his career as an evangelist, but his personal fortune was at stake. He didn't know what he was worth, but his followers, along with the press, insisted on calling him a multimillionaire. And it had been to his advantage to nurture this legend. His followers referred to his millions with personal pride. They boasted that he was richer than Father Divine, richer than Daddy Grace. Religious people love a winner, he had learned. By that they knew that God had blessed him. He rode around in a royal purple Rolls Royce with a gold plated radiator; in the winter he wore an overcoat made of ranch mink; he wore a diamond ring on each finger and diamonds in his shoes; he maintained a French-type wine cellar stocked with vintage wines and champagnes that he paraded for effect, although he never drank himself. All this might go by the board if it was discovered that the water he had blessed had poisoned one of his converts.

But he had not gotten where he was by means of a chicken heart. He had the nimble wits of a confidence man and the nerve of a bank robber. His brain worked best under pressure. "Get the bottle, Elder, get the bottle for God's sake and hide it," he said, then silenced the brass band with a gesture and spoke fervently into the microphone.

"Be calm! Be happy! Rejoice! Praise be to God! Let us all kneel in prayer. God is calling the holy ones."

The face of a big black man turned ashy gray. "I is getting the hell out of here," he muttered.

He pushed through the crowd and started running. Others followed. Terror spread through the assemblage.

"Stay and pray!" Sweet Prophet warned. "You can't run away from God."

He signaled for the band to begin playing again and raised his big bass voice in song: "Swing low, sweet chariot, coming for to carry me home . . . All sing," he commanded. "I looked over Jordan and what did I see, coming for to carry me home . . ."

Hundreds of people broke in wild flight, knocking down women and children and trampling them in the street. But the converts and the religious remained. With their drenched white dresses clinging to oversized bodies, they turned their entranced black faces toward the sky and began to sing their own individual songs.

"Oh, Jesus, I is coming . . ."

"I hear you calling me . . ."

"Call me, Jesus, I is ready . . ."

A big powerful woman clung to her husband, who was trying desperately to get away. "What's the matter with you? Don't you want to go to heaven?" she was screaming.

Tears streamed down a toothless old woman's stoic face. "Hurry, God, and take me while I is pure," she prayed.

"*Let us all kneel in prayer,*" the voice of Sweet Prophet boomed.

Automatically, as though under the influence of mass hypnotism, the multitude knelt in the street.

Sweet prophet began praying over the loud-speakers with a steady, moving fervor:

"*The Lord giveth and the Lord taketh. Ashes to ashes and dust to dust; if God doesn't get you the devil must . . .*"

No one noticed Sugar Stonewall turn the corner into Seventh Avenue and begin to run. He was a long-limbed, double-jointed

11

man with fallen arches and flat feet. He ran as though his feet were made of beef filets and the streets were paved with broken glass, using his arms, like a windmill to keep him afloat. But he was putting his heart into it. He didn't know how much he would have to do, nor how much time he would have to do it in.

2

The colored corporal in charge of the street detail rushed to the nearest police telephone box and telephoned the Homicide Bureau.

Elder Jones, at Sweet Prophet's direction, dashed to the nearest drugstore and telephoned the police precinct station for an ambulance.

Some well-meaning person telephoned the fire department.

Someone else telephoned Harlem's great undertaker, H. Exodus Clay.

It was Sunday, and all of them were delayed; but the undertaker's hearse got there first. The regular driver, Jackson, was attending the First Baptist church with his wife, Imabelle, when the call came in, so the relief driver took it.

He was a young man without much experience, but eager to make good. Mr. Clay told him to get a death certificate before bringing the body in. When he got to the scene there was no one present to give him the necessary death certificate, and he didn't have time to wait.

He grabbed the body, loaded it into the wicker basket, shoved the basket into the hearse and took off with the siren wide open before the police realized what was happening. He gripped the steering wheel in a death grip and stared at the onrushing street with a fanatical look.

The first place he went to was Harlem Hospital. They told him they couldn't give him a death certificate, but they would examine the body in the emergency receiving room and telephone the police for him.

"Hell with that!" he said. He didn't have time for all that foolishness.

From Harlem Hospital he drove furiously to Knickerbocker Hospital, also located in Harlem.

The doctors there, after listening to his request, told him he had better take the body to the morgue, where he could find an assistant medical examiner on duty who would issue the necessary certificate.

By the time the police got on the job of tracing his movements, he was heading south, down the East Side Highway at eighty-five miles an hour, making for the morgue on First Avenue at 29th Street.

Directly after the hearse had left the scene, Sweet Prophet called for his Rolls Royce, and was driven rapidly to his Temple of Wonderful Prayer around the corner on 116th Street. Anticipating all sorts of trouble from the hard-boiled Homicide police, he desired to face them on his home ground.

The others arrived consecutively:

First, two fire trucks bringing oxygen tents and inhalators;

Second, the Assistant Medical Examiner, who had been alerted by the Homicide Bureau;

And last, a big black sedan from the Homicide Bureau itself, with a uniformed driver, bearing three plain-clothes detectives, a sergeant and two corporals.

By then the body was gone, the prophet was gone, the witnesses were gone, the bottle which had contained the allegedly poisoned water was gone, and Sugar Stonewall was long gone.

Now, more than an hour had passed since Alberta Wright had swallowed the first gulps of the water from the bottle Sweet Prophet had blessed, and Sweet Prophet was sitting behind a hand-carved mahogany desk in his sumptuous "Receiving Room" on the third-floor front of his Temple of Wonderful Prayer. Across from him, in the high-backed period chairs usually assigned to the supplicants, sat three detectives. They were enclosed, as it were, by an invisible wall, behind which the room was jammed to the walls by as many of the prophet's followers as could squeeze inside. Others jammed the outside hallways and staircases, and hundreds stood below on the street.

The temple was a four-storied apartment building, housing a modern motion picture theater, which Sweet Prophet had converted into his Church of Wonderful Prayer. His living quarters were on the top floor.

The Homicide sergeant was saying, "Now all I want to do is get the picture straight while the Medical Examiner locates the body and determines the cause of death. There has been some confusion here."

"The Lord shall confound the wicked," Sweet Prophet said.

"Amen," said the followers.

The sergeant, a tall lean hatchet-faced Irishman named Ratigan, blinked. "As to that, we'll soon find out," he said. "You were baptizing these people?"

14

"They had answered to the call, and the Sweet Prophet was opening the gates to God's green pastures so that they may graze in faith with God's chosen flock," Sweet Prophet said.

"Amen," the faithful said.

"Just stick to the answers, Reverend," Sergeant Ratigan said.

"I am a prophet," Sweet Prophet said. "God called to me at the corner of this very street and Lenox Avenue more than thirty-three years ago. It was a Saturday night and the street was filled with sinners – pimps and prostitutes and thieves. God touched me on the shoulder. I looked around and saw nobody. He said, 'I am God. I make you my prophet on Earth. I send you forth to save these people from degradation and damnation!' "

"Praise be God and bless Sweet Prophet," the faithful said.

"Jesus Christ, do these people have to be here?" Ratigan said, gritting his teeth. "They are interfering with the questioning, obstructing the police and loitering, all of which is against the law."

"They are humble, very humble," Sweet Prophet said. He tossed a handful of bread crumbs onto the floor, touching off a mad scramble. "See how humble we all are," he stated to the bug-eyed detectives. "We will even eat off the floor for Sweet Prophet."

Many of the faithful were lapping the crumbs from the thick purple carpet.

"All right, all right, stop feeding them crumbs and let's get back to the killing," Sergeant Ratigan said harshly.

"There was no killing," Sweet Prophet denied. "No killing and no death. There was a departure. A saint departed for heaven."

"The question is, did any human dispatch her on her way?" Ratigan said.

"None! No human hand was raised against her," Sweet Prophet said.

"Who poisoned the bottle of water?" Sergeant Ratigan asked.

"The water was not poisoned," Sweet Prophet denied. "I blessed it with my own hand."

"How is it then that she died after drinking it?" Ratigan asked.

"If you think she died from drinking that water, bring me a gallon of it and I will drink it all," Sweet Prophet said.

"What did she do for a living?" the sergeant asked.

"She was a cook for a white family in Westchester County," Sweet Prophet said.

"What kind of woman was she?" Ratigan asked.

"An upright, God-fearing, Christian woman," Sweet Prophet said.

15

"Do you have any idea why someone might want to poison her?" Ratigan asked.

"No one would have ever wanted to poison her," Sweet Prophet stated emphatically. "She was a great cook and a steady wage-earner. No one on God's green earth would poison that type of woman."

"How about a jealous husband or a disgruntled lover?" the sergeant asked.

"Only the Almighty Father, who is swayed neither by the color of the skin nor the smartness of the brain, but judges only by the sincerity of the heart, would have called Sister Wright from her life on Earth to offer her a seat in heaven – as useful as she was to everybody," Sweet Prophet said.

One of the four gilded telephones on the desk began to ring. Sweet Prophet looked at them without moving, and a sedately dressed middle-aged woman, who had been standing impassively by the wall behind him, stepped forward and miraculously picked up the right one.

"The blessed Sweet Prophet's Temple of Wonderful Prayer," she enunciated in a well-modulated voice.

The harsh sound of a voice at the other end came into the room, but the words were indistinct.

"Very well," the woman replied and, looking up toward the sergeant, said, "It is for you, sir, if you are Sergeant Ratigan."

The sergeant got to his feet and reached across the desk for the receiver.

"Ratigan," he bellowed. "Shoot!"

The sound of the harsh voice, metallic and indistinct, poured into the dense, listening silence, punctuated by Ratigan saying, "Yeah . . . Yeah . . . Well, that's that . . ."

He hung up the receiver and said to his assistants, "Let's go."

16

3

A dilapidated moving van, minus the name of the owner or any identifying inscription save for a license plate almost obliterated by dirt, drew up in front of a four-storied brick tenement on 118th Street. The block was parallel to the one on 117th Street where the baptism had taken place a short time before.

Two big overall-clad colored men, one of whom had been driving, and a small, white-haired Jew, wearing a black suit and a brown felt hat, got out.

"Hey, auntie," the Jew called to a big black woman leaning from a first-floor window. "What floor does Rufus Wright live on?"

The woman gave him an evil look. "If you means Alberta Wright, she lives on the top floor."

The Jew's eyebrows shot upward, but he didn't reply.

"If Rufus has brought in a woman, we won't touch it," he said to his helpers as they climbed the smelly stairs.

The helpers said nothing.

On the fourth floor, a slick-looking Negro with straightened hair beckoned from the rear door and said, "Psst." He was wearing a pink sport shirt, a green silk suit and yellow linen shoes, and he had a wide, confidential grin.

The Jew and his helpers entered the parlor of a two-room flat.

The Negro closed the door and locked it, then said, "All right, daddy-O, let's get on."

The Jew looked about suspiciously. "You're alone, ain't you?" He had been around colored people so long he talked like one.

"Ain't I always?" the Negro countered.

"You know I got to get it straight."

"All right, set up your alibis."

The Jew frowned. "That's a bad word," he said, but the Negro didn't argue the point. The Jew asked, "Your name is Rufus Wright, ain't it?"

"Right," Rufus said.

The helpers, standing inside the doorway, sniggered. Every time the Jew bought anything from Rufus, he went through the same act.

"This is your place, ain't it?"

"Right."

"You own the furniture, don't you?"

"Right."

"Who is this woman, Alberta Wright?" the Jew threw in suddenly.

"Her? She's my wife," Rufus said, without batting an eye.

"Why didn't you stick to being a bachelor?" the Jew complained. "That was safer."

"Well, you see, daddy-O, this time it's different," Rufus said. "This time it's on her account that I got to sell my furniture."

"What's wrong with her?"

"Nothing wrong with her. She's dead is all. That's why I got to raise some money on a Sunday. I got to pay the undertaker some money in advance so he'll go down to the morgue and get the body."

The Jew grinned at his helpers to show he appreciated the story. "Well, that's all right," he conceded, relaxing. "Now we got everything straight." He turned again to his helpers and called them to witness. "You boys heard what Mr. Wright said."

They nodded.

"All right, Rufus boy, let's get down to business. Is that the set you want to sell?" he asked, pointing toward a huge blond-oak television set on a gate-legged table.

"I've decided to sell all my furniture," Rufus said. "This funeral is going to be expensive, and I got to make a down payment of five hundred dollars."

"For that much, you had ought to got the whole Blumstein's department store," the Jew said drily.

"There's a lot of good stuff here," Rufus contended.

The Jew looked over the room, and his expression went sour. The room was jammed with a motley collection of worn-out furnishings arranged about a potbellied stove like molting chickens about a mother hen: threadbare rugs; moth-eaten over-stuffed chairs and a sofa, broken-legged tables; clocks without works; ceramic statuettes that had been through the Inquisition; a stuffed pheasant with a bald patch on its back; a set of scarred antlers mounted on the wall, flanked by faded lithographs of English hunting scenes; cutout photos of Negro blues singers hanging beside reproductions of the Virgin Mother and Child, The Last Supper and The Crucifixion cut from calendars given out by undertaker H. Exodus Clay.

"Do you call this furniture?" the Jew asked.

"These are mostly antiques in this room," Rufus said. "But

there's a brand new set of furniture in the bedroom."

"Your wife couldn't say no to her white folks, could she?" the Jew cracked. "She must have brought everything home that they left for the trash man."

"She couldn't throw nothing away either," Rufus added.

Grinning, the Jew took a notebook and stylo from his inside coat pocket and went to work. Rapidly and with scarcely a look, he itemized the furnishings, allowing $50 for the television set and $19 for everything else.

"I can't use the stove," he said. "Sixty-nine bucks for the lot. Okay."

"You mean that's all you want to pay for everything in this room?" Rufus asked incredulously.

"That's more than it's worth," the Jew said, adding with a grin, "I wouldn't pay for it if it wasn't for your wife needing a decent funeral."

With an abrupt motion, Rufus opened his mouth and stuck it in front of the Jew's face. "Here, take my teeth too and have it done with," he blubbered.

The Jew looked into his mouth with interest. "Holy Mackerel, you got a red tongue, blue gums and white teeth," he observed. "If anybody calls you a Communist, you just open your mouth and show them the national colors."

Rufus closed his mouth and looked sheepish. "All right, sixty-nine bucks; if I got to, I got to."

The helpers started to move the furniture but the Jew stopped them. "Wait till I get it down legal," he cautioned.

In the bedroom the bureau drawers and the dressing table still contained Alberta's personal effects, lingerie and toilette articles as she had left them that morning, and the bed was made up and covered with a pink rayon spread.

"Get these drawers cleaned out," the Jew said.

Rufus began piling the contents helter-skelter in a corner of the room. The Jew went about his business of assessing the furniture without paying him the slightest attention.

When he had thrown off the bed linen to examine the mattress, the Jew said sharply, "This has been damaged."

The seams of the mattress on all four sides, both top and bottom, had been opened with a knife wide enough to permit a hand.

"I had to open it to put in some bug powder," Rufus said. "We been bothered with the bugs. But all it needs is sewing up a little and it'll look like new."

The Jew wasn't listening. He was sticking his arm through the openings and probing the padding with his fingers. With an enraged gesture, he wheeled it over to the floor and probed the other side. His face was a study of frustration.

"The deal's off," he choked in a furious voice. His sallow skin had turned the dull purple of a ripe fig.

"What the hell's the matter with you!" Rufus shouted, his eyes bugging in matching fury. "You think I'm going to sell you a mattress if there was any money hidden in it?"

"It's risky, too risky," the Jew said, halfcowed by Rufus's threatening attitude. "If money has been stolen, I won't touch it."

"What risk is you taking?" Rufus kept raving. "You don't never take no risk. It's me takes all the risks. The way you cover yourself up with all kinds of legal tetches, all of Congress couldn't get nothing on you."

The Jew gave in. "All right, all right. We don't have to fight. I just like to do my own looking, whether I find anything or not."

"Hell, you think you're going to find a bale of money in every mattress you buy," Rufus said scornfully.

It was rumored in Harlem that twenty years ago the Jew had found thirty-five thousand dollars in cash hidden in a mattress he had bought for 75c from a flea-bag hotel room in which an old white beggar had died.

Rufus kept on needling. "Us colored folks ain't got no money to hide. You Jews got it all."

The Jew was finished with it. "All right, drop it, boy. Twenty-seven fifty for what's in here, okay?"

"That's just what I mean," Rufus said. "My old lady paid two hundred seventy-five for this set less than a month ago."

"All right, stop breaking my heart – thirty-five, okay?" the Jew said.

Rufus wiped his smooth black cold-creamed face with a white silk handkerchief. "Okay, man, okay," he said harshly. "Let's get finished; I ain't got all day."

The Jew hid a vindictive smile and went into the kitchen. He took one look at the enamel-topped table and tubular stainless steel chairs with foam-rubber plastic-covered seats and said, "I can see that your wife was a cook."

He sat at the table and added up the total, allowing $13 for the kitchen's contents, exclusive of the table service and utensils. It came to $117. He then wrote a receipt on a form taken from a pad that looked like a check book:

20

Received from A. Finkelstein $117.00 for total furnishings of apartment No. 44, 118th Street, Manhattan, New York City.

Leaving it undated, he asked Rufus to sign it.

"Man, don't you never talk to me no more about taking risks," Rufus grumbled as he signed.

"You got to bury your wife," the Jew needled slyly. "I ain't got no wife."

The helpers exchanged looks and grinned.

"No cracks," the Jew warned. "You just sign here as witnesses."

Laboriously, they spelled out their signatures below.

"Okay, now you can take this junk and load it," the Jew said, tucking the receipt carefully into a stuffed wallet and extracting a thin sheaf of banknotes.

Stolidly the helpers shuffled into the sitting room and began slamming the furniture about. The colored lady had retired from her grandstand seat in the front window when they appeared on the street with the first load, but other windows up and down the street on both sides were occupied with the customary Sunday afternoon sightseers. No significance was attached to the moving. In a number of windows only the grayish bottoms of big bare black feet resting on the sills were visible from below; and they remained stationary. A patrol car idled past, but the cops didn't give the movers a second look. Moving on Sunday was a perfectly legitimate undertaking; many people figured that was the best time to do it.

The helpers loaded the bureau and the dressing table in the van alongside the sitting room suite, then, after knocking the bed apart, brought it down in sections. One of them brought down the mattress, and the other brought down the springs. They packed the springs but left the mattress on the tailgate to be used as a buffer for the stuff from the kitchen. Before going back up, they went forward to the driver's compartment and drank heartily from a bottle of California muscatel wine.

A young man standing in the doorway of the adjoining tenement sucked on a marijuana cigarette and watched them with an expression of infantile concentration. He had a big, flat body, whose wide square shoulders gave the impression of abnormal strength. He had a small head with a round babyish face and smooth brown hairless skin. His big eyes with their drug-widened pupils looked completely senseless. Despite the heat he wore a heavy tweed jacket with thick shoulder pads, a wide-brimmed beaver hat pulled low over his forehead and skintight mustard-colored corduroy pants tucked into black and white cowboy boots. On first sight he looked like a harmless moron.

As soon as the Jew's two helpers went back upstairs, he squashed the marijuana butt, stuck it into the band of his hat and sauntered toward the truck. Without looking about to see whether or not he was being watched, he shouldered the mattress as though it were stuffed with down and began walking casually in the direction of Lenox Avenue.

A young brown-skinned woman, looking out of a window as he passed her tenement lodging, laughed melodiously.

"Hey, baby, come look at this spook with his house on his back," she called over her shoulder.

A muscular black man, naked to the waist, appeared at her side. "He's probably found a new gal and he's moving in with her," he said.

The young man turned the corner at Lenox Avenue and disappeared.

When the helpers came down with the kitchen table and chairs, they noticed the mattress was missing. They looked up and down the street. The young woman saw them and shouted, "Ain't no need of looking, 'cause sleepy done got it."

"Sleepy who?" one of them asked.

"How do I know who?" she replied. "You think I knows any niggers who steals mattresses?"

The muscular man reappeared at her side, and the helpers had business back upstairs.

The Jew was sniffing about in the kitchen when they came up. Figuring he might find something good to eat, they didn't disturb him with news of the stolen mattress but hurried to get finished.

The Jew lifted the lid from a big iron pot on the stove and found it half filled with a concoction of boiled rice and squares of orange-colored meat that smelled like fish. He dished up some with his finger and tasted it. "Mmmm, it's good," he said. "What is it?"

Rufus stuck his nose in the pot and tasted a bit of the bright-colored meat. "It's alligator tails and rice," he said. "It's a great dish in South Carolina." Then he added, "That's where my wife came from."

"Rest her soul," the Jew said, took a plate from the cupboard and began serving himself.

When the two helpers finished they found their boss eating from a plate on the stove and Rufus from a plate on top of the icebox.

22

"Tails and rice," they chorused in unison and joined the feast, putting their plates on the sink.

One stopped long enough to look for some whiskey but only found a bottle of black rum behind a stack of used paper sacks on the top shelf.

"You don't mind if us drink a little of this," he asked Rufus.

"Help yourself," Rufus said.

He and the Jew drank beer.

By the time they had cleaned the pot, everybody felt lovey-dovey. It wasn't until the three of them had gone downstairs and were about to enter the van that the driver remembered to tell the Jew about the stolen mattress.

The Jew looked thoughtful. He wasn't worried about the mattress, but with everybody having the same idea, he resolved to look into the stuffings of the living room suite as soon as possible.

Rufus was thinking along the same lines. Upstairs he had taken off the locked door of the clothes closet by knocking out the pins of the hinges, and was searching inside. But he didn't find anything but clothes, two empty pasteboard suitcases, a stack of shoe boxes filled with slips containing the hit numbers for the past five years and a variety of nameless junk.

He looked as though he had been taken.

After a moment he shrugged and walked out of the flat like a man trying to play the part of a good loser. He locked the door with the key that Sugar had given him, went down the stairs and hesitated for a moment in the entrance. He didn't see anyone who seemed concerned with him, so he went down the street and around the corner and got into his car parked in the shade on Lenox Avenue.

4

On the south side, Harlem is bounded by 110th Street. It extends west to the foot of Morningside Heights, on which Columbia University stands. Manhattan Avenue, a block to the east of Morningside Drive, is one of the corner streets that screen the Harlem slums from view. The slum tenements give way suddenly to trees and well-kept apartment buildings, where the big cars of the Harlem underworld are parked bumper to bumper. Only crime and vice can pay the high rents charged in such borderline areas. That's where Rufus lived.

Sugar climbed the stairs of a modern brick building at the corner of 113th Street and knocked at the door of a second-floor apartment.

Rufus answered. He had shed his green silk jacket, but was still wearing the pants along with the pink sport shirt.

"I want to talk to you," Sugar panted menacingly.

"I got a woman inside," Rufus said. "Let's go in the park."

They went down to the street and crossed to the small triangular park formed by the converging of Morningside Drive and Manhattan Avenue at 112th Street. Across the Drive was the rocky incline of Morningside Park, filled with Sunday picnickers. They sat on a green wooden bench.

"Look here, nigger, I told you just to take the television set," Sugar said accusingly.

"You told me she had some money hid there somewhere," Rufus contended. "I searched the place and I didn't find nothing."

"Hell, do you think I didn't search it before I came for you?"

"I heard she dropped dead," Rufus said. "I had to get something for my trouble."

"You didn't have no right to take the furniture – that was mine," Sugar stated.

"If she had anything, she didn't hide it in that furniture," Rufus said. "You can take it from me, man; I have searched too many of these places to miss."

"She had something hidden there, all right," Sugar contended. "I'll bet my life on it."

Rufus looked skeptical. "You know she didn't have much sense. An ignorant woman like her always hides everything in the mattress. And there wasn't nothing in that mattress."

"She had sense enough to fool both of us so far," Sugar reminded him.

"Then she must have hid it somewhere else," Rufus said.

"Where else could she have hid it?" Sugar persisted.

"How in the hell would I know? I wasn't living with her. You was," Rufus said. "And as far as that goes, you ain't got any proof that she ever had anything."

"Oh, I got proof enough," Sugar said. "Besides which, she gave herself away."

"How?"

"Never mind how – that's my little secret."

"You mean because she locked you out of the house last night?" Rufus asked.

"Naw, man, hell, she done that lots of times before," Sugar admitted, but he didn't feel that it was necessary to explain to Rufus the source of his suspicions. He had the feeling that Rufus was smarter than he was, and he didn't want to give him too much to go on. "If you knew her as well as you claim to, you would know she must have got hold of something in order to get religion suddenly," he added.

Rufus looked thoughtful. "Maybe you're right," he conceded. "I'll go through her junk again, piece by piece."

"Where is it?" Sugar demanded.

"I ain't saying," Rufus replied. "You got your little secret; I got mine."

"All right, man, just don't get yourself hurt."

"Hell, man, I trusted you; now you got to trust me."

"I trust you – I am just telling you, is all. It's halvers."

"I know it's halvers, man. If I find it, you'll get your half, all right."

Just remember this is worth your life, man," Sugar threatened.

"You talk like a mugger," Rufus complained aggrievedly. "You don't have to threaten me, man."

"I ain't threatening you," Sugar denied. "I'm just advising you. Don't try nothing funny."

Rufus stood up. "I'm going, man, I got a chick waiting."

"Just don't get careless and find yourself dead," Sugar called after him.

5

For years, Third Avenue crossed the Harlem River a few blocks north of 125th Street on the tracks of the Third Avenue Elevated and continued northward through the Bronx to Fordham Road. Now, with the old El gone out of existence. Third Avenue simply leaps from shore to shore. On one shore the address is Third Avenue, Manhattan; on the other it is Third Avenue, Bronx. In both Manhattan and the Bronx, its character is the same. It is a street of the second-hand and the down-and-out; of pawnshops, of grimy bars, of poverty and bums – a truly democratic street.

In the block between 166th and 167th Street in the Bronx there is a grimy bar owned by a Greek with a colored bartender serving a clientele of all races; an Army-Navy surplus store; a kosher meat market; a second-hand clothing store run by the United Protestant Missions; a pork store; a store front with a name protected by a heavy iron grille strong enough to serve as the gates for Alcatraz; a big wooden gate that had once been painted yellow; and a big weather-blackened brick building housing a brewery owned by the descendants of a German immigrant.

It was ten o'clock at night. Save for an intermittent bus, scattered automobiles and a few forlorn pedestrians straggling by, the street was deserted. Only the lighted window in the brewery and the fly-specked window of the bar at the opposite end showed signs of life.

Two brass locks securing the iron grille of the nameless store gleamed dully in the feeble light from the distant street lamp. Vaguely visible in the display window behind, broken furniture was stacked to the ceiling as though to form a secondary barrier. The windows of the three floors above the store were boarded shut.

The wooden gate to one side enclosed a short brick-paved driveway leading to a wooden shed with a tin roof. Protruding from the shed was the back end of a moving van.

There was a small doorway in the back of the shed that opened onto a small concrete courtyard extending across the rear of the store. Two windows, boarded up and barred, flanked a center door that was protected by a grille similar to the one in front. But light was coming from a small basement window at ground level on the far side.

Through dirt-spattered panes a basement room was visible. One corner of the basement had been partitioned off and equipped for a cabinetmaker's workshop. Workbenches were built along three walls, above which were tool racks containing all types of wood-working tools. Near the inner wall stood a band saw, a wood lathe, a planing mill and an electric drill.

What was left of Alberta's moth-eaten overstuffed parlor suite was scattered about the center of the floor in the spill of bright white light from a green-shaded drop lamp.

The Jew was kneeling beside the sofa, which was still intact. The skeletons of the two overstuffed armchairs had been pushed to one side like the bones of a carcass. The covers and overstuffing were piled in a heap between them.

He felt the sofa as though he were assaying a prime beef, poked it here and there and then caressed it with soft loving strokes.

"Marvelous," he muttered to himself. "Marvelous. More than a hundred years old. Made in New Orleans. Been through the Civil War. Extraordinary! What treasures these black cooks collect."

Suddenly he picked up his tools and began stripping the sofa like a past master. All the while he talked to himself.

"That Rufus, what a fool. Trying to outwit Abie – ha ha."

First he pried loose all the hidden tacks.

"The mattress – colored people's strongbox, ha ha."

Then with a razor blade he ripped the seams of the outer fabric and skinned it back as though skinning an animal. Save for the sound of ripping threads and his labored breathing, it was silent as a tomb. The silence oppressed him. He talked to relieve the silence, not because the words expressed his thoughts.

"Little fortunes . . . little fortunes . . . from little fortunes big fortunes grow . . ."

Beneath the covering was a layer of horsehair, and beneath that a layer of yellowed cotton. With immaculate care, the Jew removed each layer. His nimble fingers probed and explored every inch of padding before he laid it aside.

"He was searching for something. He thinks Abie doesn't know. He thinks he has fooled Abie. The fool – ha ha . . ."

He thought he heard a sound.

"What's that!" he exclaimed.

His eyes flew to the basement window. Quick as a cat he moved

27

toward a hidden switch beneath the projecting edge of a bench and turned off the light. The small rectangular window was outlined by the almost imperceptible light of a city night. No telltale silhouette was visible. He had been holding his breath. He breathed once and listened. Only the heavy muted sounds penetrating the thick wall of the brewery disturbed the silence.

"No one in miles," he muttered.

But he did not switch the light back on yet. He felt an inexplicable nervousness – not a premonition, more a building up of tension. He walked through the darkness to the door leading to the stairs. Something brushed against his leg. Shock went through him like cold fire. He jumped to one side, feeling his hair rise from an ice-cold scalp. His hands clawed desperately along the tool rack for a weapon.

Then a cat mewed and moved forward to rub against his other leg. He looked down and saw twin ellipsoids of green light shining in the dark.

He sucked in his breath with a watery sound.

"Sheba!" he gasped. "Sheba, little pussy."

He reached down to stroke the purring black cat.

"Sheba! Little queen. You will make a corpse of old Abie yet."

He crossed the room, turned on the light and went back to work. The kitten played around his feet.

He worked absorbedly. When the padding was removed he sounded the burlap-covered wooden frame with a small wooden mallet. His ear was cocked, listening to the sound of the wood. He worked along the back of the frame down the back legs, then around to the front legs and up the sides. The arms of the frame were seemingly solid cylinders of a light white wood. The mallet made small light sounds as it tapped against the solid wood.

"Impregnable," the Jew muttered.

Disappointment showed in the creases of his face. The cat rubbed against his leg again, and he shoved it aside with a gesture of frustration.

He began tapping the other arm. Suddenly he bent his head to listen. There was a slight hollow sound beneath the mallet blows. His face lit slowly with an expression of uncontainable avarice.

The cat had withdrawn to a distance and sat washing her face with offended dignity.

The Jew knelt and examined the end of the cylinder in the bright light. It was identical with its mate, the grains of the wood unbroken as though cut from a solid beam. He exchanged his mallet for a small iron hammer and tapped the end gently, listening. Then he took a small wood chisel from the bench and began cutting a small circle. A few minutes later the plug sank in.

"Ingenious," he muttered admiringly.

He speared the plug with a gimlet and worked it out from the arm. Behind was a cylindrical opening of an inch in diameter. He probed with his finger. His expression changed to astonishment. With a pair of pincers he fished a cylindrical packet, which fitted exactly, from the opening. The outer cover was yellow oiled silk in a state of perfect preservation. He sniffed it; it smelled slightly perfumed.

He went over to the workbench, switched on another light and smoothed the packet flat. It took the shape of a plain silk pouch, closed with a flap but unsealed. He opened the pouch and extracted a neat sheaf of bright green bank notes held by a paper band. He sucked in his breath. His face was a study in emotions.

"Fantastic!" he muttered. "Brand-new."

The notes were of one-hundred-dollar bills.

Slowly his tongue came out and slid from side to side on his bottom lip.

As he counted the notes, his eyes widened. There were 1,000 hundred-dollar bills.

Suddenly he bent double, laughing as though he had suddenly gone raving crazy. He was laughing so hard he did not hear the light sound made by a shoe sole scuffling against the pavement outside the basement window.

But the cat heard. The cat stopped washing its face and stared unblinkingly at the silhouette of a man peering through the dirty panes.

The silhouette withdrew, and the cat went back to washing its face.

The Jew finally got himself under control. He straightened up and stared at the money. Saliva trickled from the corners of his mouth. He wrung his hands as though washing them. The cat stopped washing its face again and watched him silently. He patted the money. He turned it over and looked at the other side, then held one of the notes against the light.

"Incredible," he muttered.

The next instant his body went rigid. He froze in a listening attitude, his ear cocked. The unmistakable sound of an automobile started reached his ear. Before his face could form an expression the motor caught and the loud hard roar of a big truck motor racing at top speed shattered the silence. There could be no mistake. Someone had started the motor of his moving van in the shed. No one but himself had keys to the gate. Someone had broken in.

The motor raced, then was cut to idle and left running.

He stacked the money, slipped it back into the pouch, and pulled open a drawer in the workbench, moving with incredible speed. He put the pouch into the drawer and withdrew a .38 calibre Colt revolver, loaded with tracer bullets, and a large black three-cell flashlight with an oversized lamp. He switched out the light over the bench and moved quickly toward the master switch beneath the other bench. His body, once put into motion, seemed to gather speed. The black-clad figure capped with yellow-gray hair armed with revolver and flashlight gave the impression of incalculable danger.

The switch clicked faintly, and the room was plunged into darkness. But the Jew moved through the darkness as though he could see. He ran lightly on tiptoes through the open door and up the stairs. One of the stairs creaked beneath his weight, and he swore silently in Yiddish.

The staircase turned at a landing and entered the back hall of the first floor, directly beside the back door. The Jew halted for a moment to peer through the grimy panes into the back courtyard. But, coming from the bright light of his workroom, his eyes had not adjusted to the darkness. He put his ear to the pane but could hear only the sound of the idling motor.

With infinite caution he unlocked the inner door. The slight sound made by the clicking of the bolt was barely perceptible above the sound of the idling motor. The door opened soundlessly.

He waited with his face pressed to the iron grille, looking and listening. There was still only the sound of the idling motor. The Jew figured it was a trap. But he didn't know whether it was a legitimate burglar or some teenage hoodlums. He had a telephone in the ground floor cubbyhole office. He could have phoned for the police, but he didn't want the police meddling into his business, poking about and asking questions.

He decided to set a trap of his own. He unlocked the grille and pushed it back on its hinges until it formed a right angle, guarding the entrance from any attack from the left. Then he backed into the shadows and waited.

Five minutes passed. The cat came up the stairs, looked outside, sniffed and walked in a dignified manner across the couryard with its tail straight up, looking neither to the right nor the left. The Jew knew that was no indication; Sheba would simply ignore anyone she didn't know.

Ten minutes passed, then fifteen. The Jew began growing impatient. He wanted to get back to his money. It could have been some pranksters. No one in their right senses would want to steal his moving van. And had anyone wanted to get into the store, they would have made a move by now. He would wait another five minutes.

He was guessing at the time; but the clock of his mind was fairly accurate. When the five minutes had ticked off in his brain, he put the revolver beneath his coat and cocked it to muffle the sound. Then, holding the heavy black flashlight extended in his left hand, thumb on the switch, and holding the heavy revolver extended in his right hand, finger on the trigger, he emerged slowly from the dark square of the doorway.

To the right of the doorway, a man plastered to the brick wall stepped out. He had outwaited the Jew.

The Jew saw the hammer descending and moved instinctively a fraction of an instant before it struck him on the bone point of his right shoulder. His gun arm went numb with the brackish taste of bone ache. The gun went off before it fell, clattering, to the pavement. Out of the roar the bullet drew a white line through the dark against the brick wall of the brewery and ricocheted upward in a series of arabesques.

The man kicked at the gun with his left foot at the same time that he swung the hammer again with his right hand. The Jew had pressed the switch, and the light came on the instant the hammer smashed the reflector. It was as though a bolt of lightning had struck once, almost at the moment of the thunder, making the darkness blacker. The flashlight sailed from the Jew's hand and rolled across the yard. His hand and forearm were filled with pins and needles up to his elbow.

The Jew was blinded. Both arms were useless. But he kicked out viciously and caught his assailant on the shin. Grunting with pain, the assailant doubled over. The hammer blow aimed at the Jew's head struck him in the ribs. The sound of a breaking rib came like a drum beat from under water. The Jew tried to scream but didn't have the breath. His assailant swung back-handed from a one-footed stance. The blow caught the Jew over the right ear with the sound of a butcher cleaving a marrow bone. The Jew's tightly stretched mouth went instantly slack; his taut muscles went limp. He fell in a flabby heap.

31

The assailant bent over and rained blows on the prostrate figure. For a time there was only the rising and the falling of the hammer, the soft meaty sounds as it landed on the Jew's face and head.

Then suddenly it stopped.

The assailant dropped the hammer to the pavement, sat down and put his face in his hands. Inhuman sounds spewed from his mouth. He sounded as though he were crying with uncontrollable terror.

Suddenly the crying stopped.

The assailant rose to a squatting position and snapped on a cigarette lighter. In the flickering light the Jew appeared to be a bundle of bloody rags. The light snapped off quickly.

Quickly, in the dark, the assailant searched the Jew's body. He found nothing, no money, no wallet, no papers.

He had to go inside. His body shaking with terror, he couldn't find the switch. By aid of his cigarette lighter, he descended the stairs. Suddenly a stair squeaked beneath his weight. The cigarette lighter fell from nerveless fingers, and he had to grope for it in the darkness. His breath made a wheezing sound. Finally he found the lighter. It didn't work immediately. He groped his way to the bottom of the stairs and tried the lighter again. It burned, but the flame was more feeble than before.

Time was running out.

For a moment he stood in the door and looked over the room. Objects were barely discernible in the dim flickering light, but he made out the workbench where the Jew had last been seen standing. He crossed to it, put the lighter down and began snatching open drawers. He found it where the Jew had put it.

He held the oiled silk pouch in his hand as though it were as fragile as hope of heaven. His body was bent forward. His eyes were focused. His face held an expression of savage greed.

One hundred grand, he thought.

Suddenly he heard the loose stair creak.

His head was gripped in a vise of ice. It was the dead Jew coming for his money. Instinctively he whirled about, snatching up a wood chisel for a weapon. Only his stifled breathing was audible, but he could sense a presence on the stairs.

He put the pouch into his hip pocket and buttoned the flap, then snapped on his lighter, held it in one hand and the chisel in the other and tiptoed cautiously toward the door.

As he reached the door, he heard feet clatter down the stairs. His body collided with another. In the dark neither could see. He

32

stabbed out with his chisel and heard a sharp cry of pain. At the same time he felt the cool, quick, almost painless slash of a knife across his cheek. Theirs was a brief but furious struggle. He stabbed out crazily, pumping the chisel with an insensate fury. He could feel the difference when it chopped into the wall and when he made contact with cloth and flesh. He couldn't see the knife, but he knew it stabbed the air about him. He felt it enter his flesh countless times. He felt no pain, but he was crazed with terror.

On both sides there were unintelligible grunts – no more. No words were spoken. No curses uttered. Two bodies weaved and ducked and stabbed blindly in the utter darkness. Then the first one broke free and ran.

He thought he was running toward the stairs until he banged into a solid object in the dark. He bounced off, tripped over something else and fell full length onto something that felt like bed springs. He could hear the other in furious pursuit, banging into furniture and grunting like an animal.

The springs seemed to have wrapped themselves about his legs. He fought them off as though they had hands, kicking and stomping. Other objects rose from the dark and struck him in all conceivable places. Something hooked into his ear and tore the lobe. Something else chopped him squarely in the mouth. Objects clutched his ankles. It was as though the broken and dilapidated furniture had taken on life to torture him like a mob of lynchers. His pursuer was undergoing the same torture but that was no consolation.

By the time he had made a tour of the basement storeroom, he had been battered unmercifully. His breath came in sobs. He still clung to the chisel, but he scarcely had the strength to use it. Finally he encountered the stairs. He dragged himself up. He could hear his unseen assailant furiously fighting the treacherous furniture and grunting unintelligible curses in the dark.

He came out in the dark courtyard sucking for breath. His mouth ballooned with vomit, and his teeth bit together. He found the body of the dead Jew where he had left it. He felt a crazy impulse to scream at the top of his voice. He knew he was bleeding from many stab wounds, but he couldn't feel them.

The sudden silence below alerted him again. He heard the loose stair squeak loudly as a foot leaped upon it. He ran toward the shed.

The motor of the moving van was still running as he had left it. Without a loss of motion he leaped into the driver's seat. He put the big old van into reverse, raced the motor and released the clutch. It

33

backed into the gate like a battering ram. The gate broke from its hinges and sailed across the sidewalk into the middle of Third Avenue. The truck followed.

He pulled the emergency brake from force of habit and was running before he hit the ground.

6

Morningside Park is one of those rocky jungles on the uninhabitable eastern edge of the stone ridge forming the bluffs overlooking the Hudson River. For the most part it is overgrown with dense foliage and interlaced with steep winding stairways, upon which none but the simple-minded dare to venture after dark.

Shortly after midnight, patrol cars converged on that area of the park near the bench where Sugar had met Rufus that afternoon.

There had been an anonymous report to the precinct station that a man was heard screaming there.

But by the time the first of the patrol cars arrived, the screaming had ceased. Drops of dark blood led from a flashy green sedan parked at the curb. There were blood splotches on the back of the driver's seat and on the steering wheel. The drops grew into heavy blobs on the sidewalk leading toward the darkness of a public lavatory and the black-dark jungle of the park beyond. The lavatory was closed and locked for the night, and the trail of blood led around it into the overgrown foliage. Police flashlights stabbed the pools of darkness in the dense undergrowth.

The usual Harlem crowd had collected on the sidewalk and the street, and the cops had difficulty keeping them back.

"Here it is!" a cop announced.

It was curled deep within a clump of shrubbery where it had crawled to hide.

"Stand back! Get back!" a police corporal ordered.

"I know him; I knows that man," a big black man in working clothes said excitedly. "He be George Clayborne."

"And who be you?" the corporal asked.

"I be the janitor of that there house across the street. That there is where George Clayborne lives."

"Take his name," the corporal ordered; he seemed to have put himself in charge. "Get a statement; and the rest of you get some statements from these other people. We can't do no more until the Medical Examiner and the Homicide men arrive."

"That be his car there," the janitor informed the young cop who was taking his statement.

The cop opened the front door and found what looked like bloodstains on the steering wheel and front seat.

He shouted for the corporal.

A skinny little black girl, with ribbon-tied braids sticking out from her head at all conceivable angles, looked about carefully until she found the biggest cop. She sidled up and tugged his sleeve.

He gave a start and clawed at his pistol. All these wild-looking colored people had set his nerves on edge. When he saw who had touched him, he turned bright red.

"What do you want?" he shouted angrily.

The little girl looked up at him through big brown solemn eyes. "I seen who done it," she said.

The big cop gave another start. "What?" He wasn't sure he had heard right.

"It was a white lady. I seen her with the knife."

"White lady!" The big white cop rejected that. "Go home and go to bed; you don't know what you're talking about."

"I seen her with the knife," the little girl insisted. "It had blood all over it, and she was all in white like a ghost."

"What's that?" the big slow-witted cop barked. "You mean dressed in white. Then she wasn't no white lady."

"Nawsuh, she were just dressed in white, is all," the little girl said stolidly. "I seen which way she went."

"Come on, we'll get after her," the big cop said, all for action. "We'll go in the car and you show us which way she went."

He pushed his way through the crowd to his car, where his partner sat behind the wheel, smoking.

"This little girl saw the murderer," he said. "She's going to show us where she went."

They put the little girl between them. She pointed down 112th Street toward Eighth Avenue.

The car roared down the long block with the siren wide open and burst into Eighth Avenue at sixty miles an hour.

The little girl craned her neck and pointed suddenly toward a white-clad figure walking rapidly down Eighth Avenue in the direction of 110th Street. "There is she!" she cried.

The patrol car was half way across the avenue, traveling at the speed of one mile a minute. The driver stood on the brakes and wheeled the car at a sheer right angle as though piloting a supersonic jet plane in an open sky. The scream of tires blended with the scream of the siren, and a northbound car on Eighth

36

Avenue sheered off to the left side of the street and crashed head on into a southbound car, which was sliding sidewise on locked brakes as a result of the patrol car crossing in front of it. The patrol car hit the curb broadside with the edges of its wheels, started turning over, scraped against an iron light post that knocked it back on four wheels, hit a row of garbage cans and knocked them across the wide sidewalk through the plate glass windows of a supermarket. The crash of metal on metal and tin against glass rended the night with ear-splitting sound, and people were seen to duck for cover as far away as Seventh Avenue.

Across the street the white-clad figure started to run, but the patrol car hadn't stopped moving. It slued across the street, the driver bleeding from a gash in his cheek caused by broken window glass, and shimmied to a shaky stop alongside the running woman.

The cops were out and on the street before the car stopped, and the big cop made a running tackle and brought the woman down. She landed on her right thigh, kicking back with her left heel, and caught the cop smack in the mouth. By the time the other cop had rounded the car, she was getting to her feet, and she greeted him with a backhanded blow in the eye.

She was a big strong woman, as quick as a cat, and she fought the two cops as though she had gone stark raving crazy.

The quick crowd gathered as usual, and they saw a good fight.

Finally the cops got her flat on her stomach with her hands crossed behind her. The big cop sat astride her legs and the driver knelt on her neck while they snapped on the handcuffs. Before letting her up, they searched her, to the delight of the spectators, and found two knives in her uniform pocket.

One of the knives was sticky with coagulated blood.

They released her and stood up, standing away at a respectful distance as she scrambled to her feet.

"Why did you do it?" the big cop barked.

"Do what?" she asked sullenly.

If evil looks could have killed, both cops would have dropped dead in their tracks.

"Kill him," the big cop persisted.

"Kill who?" she said.

"This is the knife," the driver stated.

"What knife?" she said.

"Give me the knife," the big cop said to the driver. "You're dripping your own blood on it."

The driver passed him the knife. He wrapped it in his handkerchief.

Intense black faces watched this performance with profound interest.

The big cop decided on a new tactic. "What did you run for, then?"

"Everybody was running," she said. "I thought the world was coming to an end."

"Resisting arrest," the big cop went on. "Why did you do that if you're not guilty? The police are your friends."

This got a well-deserved laugh from the appreciative audience, but both she and the cop were in dead earnest.

"How did I know you was the cops?" she said. "I heard the noise and thought the judgment day was here; and somebody grabbed me by the legs. I thought it were the devil. You'd resist, too, if the devil had you by the legs on judgment day."

"You're not that simple-minded," the big cop said. "Come on, let's take her in," he said to the driver.

By then the patrol cars had moved over from Morningside Drive, and screaming people were running down the streets toward the scene of the new excitement.

"I doubt if this car will run," the driver said.

"Here comes the wagon, anyway," the big cop announced, pointing toward the Black Maria pushing through the crowd.

The drivers of the wrecked cars were complaining to the corporal.

"Sue the city," he advised them.

Residents were helping themselves to provisions from the smashed showcase of the supermarket. The stone-blind cops didn't see a thing.

"Where's that little girl who fingered this suspect?" the driver asked. "We need her as a witness."

The big cop looked about but didn't see her. "Jesus Christ, why did you let her go?" he asked accusingly.

"Me let her go!" the driver exclaimed indignantly. "You let her go as much as me."

"I was occupied subduing this suspect," the big cop said.

"Hell, what do you think I was doing?" the driver demanded. "Here, look at my eye."

"Okay, okay," the big cop said.

They searched among the crowd for the little girl and inquired for her, but without success. So they took the woman to the station without the little witness.

Photographs had been taken of the body in the bush, and it had been dragged into the lavatory for further examination. Its clothes had been removed.

"I find nineteen stab wounds about the head, neck, shoulders and back," the Medical Examiner said. "We can more or less say that was the cause of death."

The sergeant from the Homicide Bureau looked at the grim object laid out on the tiled floor and felt slightly nauseated.

"He looks as though he were beaten up, too," he observed.

The two plain-clothes men and the uniformed cops gathered about stared silently.

The Medical Examiner wiped his hands with a cloth dampened with alcohol.

"Yes, that's the strange thing," he admitted. "He was severely beaten with some sort of blunt instrument at least half an hour before he was killed. But notice – all of the bruises are on the front of the body, but are not concentrated in any one area like the stab wounds. There are bruises from the shins to the forehead, as though he were beaten while lying on his back."

"Somebody didn't like him," the sergeant said.

"Offhand I would say that both the stab wounds and bruises were inflicted by more than one person," the M.E. said. "But we can judge better after the autopsy whether more than one knife was used."

"You think it was a gang killing, then?" the sergeant asked.

"Either that, or the murderer was an exceedingly quick and powerful person."

"Well, a woman has been found with a bloodstained knife," the sergeant said. "And from what I've heard of the report turned in by the arresting officers, she fills the bill as quick and powerful."

The M.E. looked skeptical. "In my experience with womenfolk, I've never come across any that quick and powerful," he said.

"Well, we're going to see soon," the sergeant said.

The M.E. went toward his car, shaking his head; the sergeant went toward his car, his head on tight as a nut.

7

The sergeant was named Frick. He was a lean, black-haired man who suffered secretly from stomach ulcers. He looked now as though one of the ulcers had suddenly bitten him.

"Did you say your name was Alberta Wright?" he asked incredulously.

The woman, sitting on the stool in the cone of light that spilled from the 300-watt lamp, replied sullenly, "Yassuh, that's what I said."

The sergeant looked from the face of one of the colored detectives flanking him to the face of the other.

"Did you hear her?" he demanded.

"What about it?" Grave Digger Jones asked politely.

He stood like a farmer resting on his plow, his big, slack frame in the dark, wrinkled suit at a slouching ease.

"Yesterday around noon a call came into the bureau that she'd dropped dead at some kind of a religious festival," the sergeant said.

"She looks alive enough now," Coffin Ed Johnson remarked.

He stood on the other side of Sergeant Frick. In all but his face he was the counterpart of Grave Digger. But his acid-scarred face, the memento of an acid-throwing rumpus one night in a shanty on the Harlem River further uptown, looked like the mask of an African witch doctor.

They were both precinct detectives, but the Homicide sergeant had asked them to take part in the interrogation.

The sergeant looked down at the woman as though he expected her to take sudden flight. But she seemed attached to the stool, which was bolted to the middle of the bare floor in the sound-proof, windowless room in the Harlem precinct station known to the underworld as the Pigeon's Nest. She still wore the dirt-blackened white maid's uniform and white rubber bathing cap in which she had been baptized.

"You're giving the Homicide Bureau a hard way to go," the sergeant said. "Yesterday you were dead, and now here you are alive and killing someone else."

"I ain't been dead, and I ain't killed nobody," Alberta denied.

"All right, all right, start lying," the sergeant said. "Tell me all that happened.

She talked in the flat, whining voice she reserved for white persons who questioned her.

When she had finished talking, the sergeant said, "You took me at my word, didn't you?"

"Nawsuh, what I told you is the truth," she maintained.

The sergeant looked again at the colored detectives. "Do you believe that fairy tale?" he asked in the direction of the police stenographer, who had taken it all down, at his small desk in one corner.

The police stenographer said nothing.

"Some of it," Grave Digger said.

Beneath a battered felt hat his dark, lumpy face flickered with secret amusement. He understood the art of lying.

"Take some, leave some," Coffin Ed supplemented.

The sergeant looked as though he had been given a big dose of castor oil. He turned back to Alberta and demanded, "Let me hear that again. Maybe I didn't hear it right the first time."

"Hear what again?" Alberta asked. "You mean tell you all over again what I just told you?"

"No, just tell me that part about your finding the knife," the sergeant said. "We'll get back to the rest when we get that clear."

She took a deep breath and wiped the sweat out of her eyes. "It ain't nothing to get clear," she began apathetically. "It were just like I said. I were sitting on a bench in Central Park –"

"Doing what?" the sergeant interrupted.

"I were resting."

"By yourself?"

"Yassuh, by myself. And I seen this patrol car go past on a Hundred Tenth Street and turn into Manhattan Avenue."

"What time was it?"

"I don't know. I didn't have no watch, and I weren't interested in the time. Why don't you ask them what was driving the car?"

"I have. Just answer my questions. What happened then?"

"I had a premonition."

"Premonition of what?"

"I don't know of what. Just a premonition, is all."

"How did you feel? Faint? In a daze? Clairvoyant? Or what?"

"I felt just like I always feel when I has a premonition – like something bad was going to happen."

"To who?"

"I didn't have no feeling about who it was going to happen to."

"Do you have them every time you see a police patrol car?"

"Nawsuh. I has them about lots of things. I don't know why I has them. Some folks say I got second sight."

"You didn't have one just before the police arrested you, did you?"

"Nawsuh."

"That's too bad for you. All right, go ahead, what happened when you had your premonition?"

"I got up and followed the patrol car."

"You said before that you ran after it," the sergeant corrected.

"Yassuh, I ran," Alberta admitted. "Wasn't no use of dallying around. Premonitions don't last forever."

"What did you expect to happen?"

"I didn't know what to expect. Just something bad, is all. Something told me I ought to be there."

"Be where?"

"Where it happened."

"Why you? Why should you be there? What did you have there? Who did you know there?"

"I don't know. The ways of the Lord are mysterious. I don't question them like you does. I had a premonition and I ran after the patrol car, and that's all there is to it."

"The way in which you keep carrying on about the Lord, I feel as if He's right here in this room," the sergeant commented sarcastically.

"He is," Alberta replied solemnly. "He's right here by my side."

"All right," the sergeant said. "So what happened when you got there?"

"When I got there I saw a crowd of people and policemens gathered around. I asked a woman what happened. She said some man was killed. I asked her who it were. She said she didn't know. I asked her how he were killed. She said he were stabbed to death."

"Who did you expect it to be?" sergeant asked abruptly.

"I didn't expect it to be nobody."

"All right, so when you got there somebody slipped you the knife. Who was it?"

"Ain't nobody done no such thing and I ain't said nobody did," she replied angrily. "I stepped on something, and, when I looked down to see what it were, I seen it were a knife all covered with blood."

42

"Where was that?"

"It were in the gutter."

"Exactly where?"

"In front of the playground."

"And you tried to conceal it because you knew who had used it," the sergeant charged harshly.

But Alberta was not intimidated. "Nawsuh, I didn't do no such thing," she contradicted heatedly. "It were just like I said before – suddenly the Lord tapped me on the shoulder and told me to take the knife and throw it into the pond in Central Park and I would save an innocent man's life."

"How?"

"By throwing the knife in the pond, that's how."

"All right, who was the innocent man?"

"The Lord didn't say."

"Well, ask Him, then," the sergeant snapped. "You say He's right there by your side."

"Yassuh," she replied imperturbably, and turned and spoke to the emptiness. "Lord, who were it?"

The stenographer stopped writing and looked up sharply. For a space of time no one spoke.

Then the sergeant asked sarcastically, "What did He say?"

"He said He weren't going to tell," Alberta replied stolidly.

The police stenographer giggled, but the faces of Grave Digger and Coffin Ed remained impassive.

Sergeant Frick looked at them and rubbed the palm of his hand violently across his forehead. Every time he came to Harlem on a case he got a violent headache.

"What is it you believe about this fairy tale?" he asked the colored detectives.

"What she said she did is probably true," Grave Digger replied. "Why she did it is another story."

"Do you mean to say you believe anybody is stupid enough to try to hide a murder weapon from the police without even knowing who the murderer is?" the sergeant said incredulously.

"Sure," Coffin said. "I believe it. Not that this woman is doing that, but there are people in Harlem who will."

"Why, for Christ's sake?"

"Most people in Harlem consider the police as public enemies," Grave Digger elaborated. "But no doubt this woman has a good notion of who the murderer is."

"That's what I think," the sergeant said, then turned back to

Alberta and shot the question. "When was the last time you saw George Clayborne?"

"I ain't never heard of him," she denied.

"He was a crony of your husband's," the sergeant ventured.

"He were?" she said unconcernedly, ignoring the bait. "Do tell!" The sergeant colored.

"What did you say your husband's name was?"

"I didn't say, but, if you wants to know, he's named Rufus Wright."

"Where does he work?"

"I don't know and I don't care. I ain't seen him in nearmost a year, and what he do don't interest me."

"Who is your man?" Grave Digger asked.

"My man! He named Sugar Stonewall."

"What was he doing at Clayborne's house?" the sergeant slipped in cleverly.

"He ain't been there," Alberta maintained doggedly. "He left for Detroit on the nine-fifteen, like I said."

"No, he didn't," the sergeant said. "He was waiting for Clayborne in front of Clayborne's house when Clayborne came home. He had some business to transact with Clayborne. You were waiting in the park for Stonewall to come and tell you the outcome of the business. When you saw the patrol car pass you knew something had gone wrong. You rushed to the scene. When you found out that Clayborne had been killed, you knew Stonewall had killed him. You found the knife Stonewall had thrown away. You recognized it. You knew it could be traced to Stonewall. That's why you were going to throw it into the lagoon. All right, why did Stonewall kill him?"

"If you know all that what you asking me for?" Alberta said stubbornly.

"I'm just trying to make it easy for you," the sergeant said. "I sympathize with you," he went on, looking as sympathetic as an executioner. "I don't want to see you take the rap for a no-good man who runs away leaving you holding the bag."

"He ain't left me holding nothing," she contradicted doggedly. "Sugar Stonewall wouldn't kill a fly."

"Why weren't you at home?" Coffin Ed asked.

"I told you why. I were lonesome with Stonewall gone. I just walked down to the park and watched the young folks boating in the pond. I had just set down to rest when I seen the patrol car pass."

"Alberta, I am damn tired of listening to your lies," the sergeant said. "I am going to book you on suspicion of murder and keep you in solitary confinement until you decide to tell the truth."

"The Lord will be with me," she said defiantly.

"I am going to put out a reader for this man, Sugar Stonewall," the sergeant informed the colored detectives. "And I will wire the Detroit police, too. I want you fellows to check this woman's story."

"Right," Grave Digger said. He waited until the police stenographer had followed the sergeant from the room, then turned to Alberta and said invitingly, "Now that we are all colored folks here, you can tell us the story and let's get it over with."

"I done told all there is," she maintained stubbornly.

"Okay, we'll find out," he said roughly. "Where are the keys to your flat?"

"How do I know," she muttered. "They took them at the desk."

"Let's lock her up," Coffin Ed grated. "She's getting on my nerves."

"Get up," Grave Digger said.

They took her out and turned her over to the matron.

8

Half an hour later they had searched her flat and found it empty. They started to leave the building, on their way back to question her again.

"Pssst!" the big fat lady who lived on the first floor of the tenement on 118th Street hissed from her front window.

It was past one o'clock, and the street was deserted. Not a window was lit. Only the rats were in evidence, scavenging among the loaded garbage cans; and the hunting cats watching them from dark corners with baleful eyes.

Grave Digger jerked his thumb toward a vaguely visible outline of a female half filling the lower part of a black-dark window. Coffin Ed nodded.

"Come inside," the woman whispered. "I got something to tell you."

They turned and re-entered the dimly lit hall.

"Never look a stool pigeon in the mouth," Grave Digger said in a low voice.

Coffin Ed loosened his long-barreled, nickel-plated .38 caliber revolver in its oiled shoulder holster. Grave Digger noticed the gesture and thought, *A burned child fears fire.* He tightened with trepidation. He wondered if Coffin Ed would ever get over the memory of the acid splashing into his face. It had left him trigger-happy; and a trigger-happy detective was as dangerous as a blind rattlesnake.

To the right, a door opened cautiously a crack and then opened fully into a black-dark room.

"Get some light on," Coffin Ed grated, the revolver flashing suddenly in his hand.

"Easy does it," Grave Digger said.

A gasp was heard from the darkness, and a light came on suddenly. "Lord God, you scared me," the big fat black woman moaned. "I just didn't want nobody to see me talking to the cops."

They stepped inside, and Coffin Ed kicked the door shut behind him, holding the revolver loosely at his side. The fat lady rushed to the front window and drew the shades.

They were standing in the parlor. She offered them whiskey, which they declined.

She said with an air of secrecy, "I saw you when you came, and I knew you were going up to Alberta Wright's."

"What's happened up there?" Grave Digger asked.

The fat lady's eyes widened. "Don't you know? Her furniture was stolen while she was away at the baptism."

The detectives became suddenly alert.

"I bet you were sitting in your window with a grandstand seat," Coffin Ed said.

"I didn't see them take it away, but I saw them when they come with the moving van," she admitted.

"All right, let's have it," Grave Digger said. "And, if you are a friend of Alberta's, you'll give it to us straight."

"Lord, that child is just like a daughter to me," she said, then went on to tell with great relish the events leading up to the theft of the furniture.

"What did this Rufus Wright look like?" Grave Digger asked.

She described him as though she had been his valet.

"And Alberta knew who he was when you told her?"

"Oh, she knew him all right," the fat lady said. "Do you reckon they is relations?" She licked her lips as though it tasted good. "Maybe he's her husband; I know that other nigger ain't."

"Maybe," Grave Digger said. "You keep on watching, and if you see anything else, you call the precinct station and ask for one of us. You know who we are, don't you?"

"Lord, if I didn't know, I could guess," she said, watching Coffin Ed slip the long-barreled revolver back into its oiled shoulder holster.

She was back in her front window before the small, battered, black sedan, with Grave Digger at the wheel and Coffin Ed beside him, pulled away from the curb.

They returned to the precinct station and got on the telephones.

Coffin Ed called the morgue and got a description of the corpse and the clothes it had been wearing at the time of death. He then called the downtown Homicide Bureau, got Sergeant Frick on the phone and asked him to send up a photograph of the corpse; but he knew he wouldn't need it. Now he knew the corpse's other name was Rufus Wright.

Grave Digger telephoned the Bronx police to get a line on the location of the Jew's warehouse. He got more than he had expected.

After they had pooled their information, they reached an unspoken accord.

"We had better slip her out the back way," Coffin Ed said. "The lieutenant won't like it."

Grave Digger smiled. "Her and her private God."

They drove, with Alberta between them, crosstown toward the Harlem River. In that section of Park Avenue in back of the 125th Street Station, prostitutes and muggers lurked in the dark shadows of the stanchions of the railway trestle, waiting to take some sucker's money – or his life.

"Where are you taking me?" Alberta asked finally.

"To get your furniture that Rufus stole," Grave Digger replied.

She didn't say another word.

They crossed over on the Ellis Street Bridge and picked up Third Avenue in the Bronx at the subway junction at 149th Street.

When they came to the Jew's warehouse, the moving van was parked at the curb and the wooden gate had been leaned against the iron grille of the store front.

Two uniformed cops were on duty, and a patrol car was parked across the street.

"We're from Harlem," Grave Digger said.

"Yeah, the inspector telephoned us you were coming," one of the harness bulls said.

They took Alberta round to the back door and down into the basement room.

"There was more than this," she said.

"Look around," Coffin Ed suggested.

They turned on all the lights and watched her search the basement, then the whole main floor. She seemed more interested in mattresses than in anything else. When she had finished she asked, "Ain't there no place else?"

"This is all," Grave Digger said.

Tears welled up in her eyes.

"What is it you're looking for?" Coffin Ed asked.

But she didn't say. All she said was, "The Lord is going to make them pay for this."

"If they haven't paid now, they never will," Grave Digger said, "The Jew has been murdered, too."

Her dark face turned slowly gray.

"The Lord struck them dead," she said.

"Not the Lord," Grave Digger corrected. "Somebody down

here. Do you want to tell us about it now?"

"I want to talk to my preacher," she said.

"Well, you had better have him get in touch with your friend, The Lord," Grave Digger suggested. "You are going to need Him."

They took her back to the precinct station and had her transferred downtown to the city jail.

9

Sugar stood beside a felt-covered kidney-shaped table in a room back of a grocery store on Lenox Avenue near 118th Street, watching the stud poker game.

"What time is it?" he asked the game keeper.

The game keeper pulled out an old-fashioned Elgin watch.

"Twenty-eight minutes and fifty-seven seconds past two o'clock," he replied, gold crowns flashing as he talked.

"I got to go," Sugar said.

"What's stopping you?" the game keeper asked.

Sugar picked his way through the dark store, and the door keeper let him out into the street.

He hurried back toward Eighth Avenue, warily approaching the scene where Alberta had been arrested. The crowds had disappeared, and the dark street was practically deserted.

The wrecked cars had been pushed to the curb, and a lone patrolman guarded the supermarket. Otherwise the coast was clear. He found a colored man who had witnessed the rumpus sitting on a tenement stoop, as though waiting for something else to happen. The man told him the cops had found the murder knife on the lady they arrested.

Sugar couldn't figure that one. He knew she hadn't killed him, but what was she doing with the knife? He couldn't think of a single reason. But that could wait. Whatever she was doing with it didn't make any difference now. It spelled trouble, big trouble with a capital T.

He felt in his pocket for a cigarette. He didn't have any. He was hungry, but he didn't have the price of a feed. He didn't know anybody he could borrow so much as half a dollar from. The jokers he played tonk with didn't have any more than he had ordinarily, and that was only what their women gave them; and he knew they wouldn't lend him any if they had. He didn't have anything valuable enough to sell. He didn't have the talent to pick pockets, if there had been anybody's pocket to pick. He didn't have the nerve to rob anybody. He wasn't strong enough to mug. He hadn't made any connections with other women since he had had Alberta; he had been too lazy. He was a naturally lazy man.

And now he didn't even have any place to sleep, as tired and worn out as he was, having been up all the night before and running around all day long.

That was when he came to realize how much Alberta meant to him.

There was no need now of thinking about ways and means of stealing her money.

The main thing now was to get his woman back. Let her do the worrying. She'd find them some place to stay and something to eat. She might even find her money back. She was a strong, resourceful woman. He could depend on her.

But it would take money to get her out on bail.

He thought of Cassie. She was another kitchen slave, like Alberta. If she could afford to keep that Dummy in chips, maybe she had something cached away. And she and Alberta were such good friends maybe she would dig some of it up.

He went over to Cassie's on 112th Street, but nobody answered.

He stood in the street, feeling low and disgusted. Harlem was rough, he thought. If you didn't have money, you didn't have friends. He thought of the time he had been in jail down South. He had seen a hungry rat lapping up red pepper and sitting in a pan of water to keep its stomach cool.

He saw a man coming from the direction of Seventh Avenue. As the man came nearer Sugar saw that he was big, and wearing an old cap and clean starched overalls. But Sugar's eyes lit on the lunch pail the man was carrying. If he had had a knife, he would have tried to mug the man for his lunch. But he hadn't been able to borrow a knife. No one had been willing to lend him a knife. It wasn't what he might have done with it; it was just that nobody wanted to be without a knife. It wasn't that people wanted to use their knives on other people; it was just that they wanted to have their knives in case other people started cutting on them.

The big workman passed, keeping at a distance, his free hand in his pocket gripping his knife. Not that he suspected Sugar of any bad intentions; he just wanted to be prepared.

Sugar's feet started moving him in the direction of home. It was empty; the furniture was gone; the door was locked; his woman was in jail; and what was more the home didn't belong to him, and he didn't have the key. But it was home, the only one he had.

"Pssst!"

51

He came near jumping out of his skin.

The big fat black lady was invisible in the dark window.

"Who that?" he asked in a frightened whisper.

She came closer, and he could make out the whites of her eyes in the dim light from the distant street lamp.

"It's me – Miz Teabone."

"Hell," Sugar said evilly. "Why don't you go to bed."

"The police been here looking for you," she informed him in a stage whisper.

"Looking for me?" He was ready to light out and run a crooked mile.

"Grave Digger and Coffin Ed," she whispered theatrically. "Where's your woman?"

"She's in jail."

"I knowed it," Mrs Teabone said triumphantly. "When I heard over the radio that a Jew-man named Abie had been killed up in the Bronx, I knowed she done it. I got second sight."

"The Jew!" Sugar exclaimed. "He dead?"

"He ain't alive," she said juicily. "She beat his head in with a hammer."

"She didn't do it," he said loyally. "It must have been somebody else."

"You is the only other somebody else," she said.

Again his feet got the message before it arrived at his brain. He was running. He didn't know where he was going, but he was on his way.

Something came up fast behind him and grabbed him by the sleeve. It sounded like a winded animal. His scalp rolled. It was late at night, he was alone on the street and he didn't have a knife. He tried to put on speed. He was afraid to look around.

"Let go!" he gasped in terror.

The thing tightened its grip and pulled up beside him. They turned the corner into Lenox Avenue, neck and neck. The thing grunted urgently. He looked about and saw a gaping mouth circled with even white teeth in a broad flat face. But behind the teeth was a gaping black hole where normally a tongue should have been.

"Dummy!" he exclaimed, panting.

He stopped and sucked in air.

"Jesus Christ, man, don't scare me like that," he complained.

Dummy kept grunting. His soft brown eyes, peering out from beneath knobs of scar tissue, were urgent.

"Man, stop making those noises," Sugar said.

Dummy clutched his hand and stuck a dirty scrap of writing paper in it.

Sugar took it and turned to let the light fall over his shoulder.

He read: *the mens wants you/lay low/go to mammy stormy/she safe.*

He looked up.

Dummy's head jerked anxiously up and down.

He nodded and said, "Okay."

Dummy grinned, and his mouth looked like an exhibit of dental plates.

He was a short, heavy-set Hawaiian-looking man with thick, gray-shot, curly hair. His coarse, lumpy face was interlaced with tiny scars. He had cauliflowers for ears and pile hammers for hands. Muscles bulged from his dark brown T-shirt, but fat put him in the heavyweight division. He might have been any age from thirty to fifty.

He made an *O* with his right thumb and forefinger and turned down Lenox toward 116th Street. Sugar watched him for a moment. He had the half-sliding, bent-over gait of a full-grown gorilla.

Sugar wondered how he knew the police were looking for him. Where did he come into the story? What was his pitch? Did he know about the money?

On sudden impulse he decided to follow Dummy. But it wasn't easy. Dummy kept looking to both sides and over his shoulder with the instinctive caution of a man who can't hear. Sugar stepped into a doorway and let Dummy turn the corner into 116th Street. Then he ran after him in his high-kneed, churning, double-jointed gait.

He rounded the corner just in time to see Dummy disappear into the shadows beneath the entrance to Sweet Prophet's Temple of Wonderful Prayer.

Mammy Stormy's was over on Seventh Avenue near 115th Street. If Dummy saw him walking down 116th Street, he would naturally figure he was on his way to Mammy Stormy's. But if Dummy had gone into the Temple, he would soon know.

Above a narrow entrance, wedged between a dismal grocery store and a curtained hair-dressing parlor, was a small sign hanging in a glass box with the faintly discernible word: *Hotel*. At night the hotel entrance served the resident prostitutes as a sentry box and transient drunks as a water closet. During the day dogs dropped in to find out what the neighboring dogs had been eating.

As Sugar approached, a teenage girl came down the steep flight of stairs. Her cotton dress was rumpled and torn, and her straightened hair was mussed and stuck out from her skull like a mangled cactus plant. She was a thin girl, with small breasts, and her thin black face was wet with tears and ugly from crying.

Dummy came quickly from the entrance to the Temple and trotted across the street. Sugar kept coming toward them, trying to look as though it wasn't any business of his.

"He Georgiaed me," the girl told Dummy hysterically. "He sent me to Georgia."

Sugar couldn't help but hear her. He knew she meant that a man she had taken to her room had shown her some money, but afterwards had refused to pay her. He was surprised to learn that Dummy was trying to pimp.

Dummy told the girl to shut up with sign language, but she didn't understand. She thought he didn't understand what she was trying to tell him. she tried to demonstrate with gestures how the man had used her and put her out of the room without paying her.

"You ought to lay for him and rob him," she said. "He got a big roll of money; I saw it."

Dummy grabbed her and shook her, trying to make her hush. He didn't want Sugar to know what was happening. But the girl thought he was going to beat her because she had let herself be cheated.

"Don't beat me," she begged. "I'll help you. We can both rob him easy; he ain't got nothing but a knife."

Dummy pushed her back into the hotel entrance. She fell on the stairs and didn't try to get up. In his excitement he was trying to talk. The sounds made Sugar's flesh crawl.

Dummy took a dirty scratch pad and a pencil stub from his hip pocket and scrawled hurriedly: *git goin man / the gunmens be here soon*, and gave it to Sugar.

"How do you know the cops is looking for me if you been here all night with this chippy whore?" Sugar asked suspiciously.

Dummy wrote, *they found the knife you throwed away on alburda*. Sugar's eyes popped. "The knife I throwed away! What knife?" Dummy wrote: *the one you stabbed rufus with*.

"Man, Jesus Christ, look here," Sugar began, but Dummy grabbed him by the arm and pointed.

At the end of the block the dim lights of a small black sedan were turning slowly into 116th Street. It was now close to four o'clock.

A gargling sound issued from Dummy's mouth as he tried desperately to talk. But Sugar got the message anyway. From that distance he couldn't recognize the car nor see the faces of its occupants. But only Grave Digger Jones and Coffin Ed Johnson could raise that look on Dummy's face.

The only way to go without being seen was up the stairs. Sugar leaped over the huddled figure of the little prostitute and started quickly up the steep flights of stairs. Dummy stuck a foot inside and kicked the girl, and she jumped to her feet and followed Sugar.

"Ain't you coming, too," Sugar called softly down the stairs.

But Dummy sprinted across the street and vanished in the shadows of the entrance to the Temple.

10

Grave Digger and Coffin Ed had what they called their "stool pigeon route," which took them through the congested slum area of Harlem known as The Valley. Whenever possible they covered this route in the early hours of morning, shortly before going off duty, and contacted their stool pigeons.

Each stool pigeon had a place of contact and a time. They were not expected to show up every night, because neither did the detectives; but, if they missed three nights straight running, it was their little hip pockets, as they say in Harlem, which meant they were in trouble. Care was taken that no stool pigeon ever got to know another stool pigeon.

When they showed in their battered black sedan, idling slowly along the street, the stool pigeon at his post would give the signal. The signal was for him to cut whatever he was doing and duck into the nearest doorway, as though he were ducking the cops. After which the detectives would turn into the first dark street and park unobtrusively in the shadows with the lights cut. Then wait. Sometimes the stool pigeon could make it in a few minutes. Sometimes it took more than a half hour. The stool pigeon had to be given time to shake his companions and make a clean getaway. There was no sense in having a stool pigeon who was known to be a stool pigeon.

After returning from the Bronx with Alberta Wright, the detectives got on their route. They needed information about Rufus and the Jew. The Medical Examiner's report, photographs, fingerprints, the findings of the criminal laboratory and all the results of modern police techniques – including police theories – were generally useless in solving murders in Harlem. Interrogations helped but little because the criminal and lower-class elements of Harlem were for the most part natural-born and highly talented liars. Third-degree methods were useful, but they couldn't beat the truth out of everybody. If there were no eyewitness accounts, the detectives had to depend on stool pigeons.

On this case, they didn't know where to start. The Jew had been killed for robbery. That was the only reason that particular Jew would ever be killed, they reasoned. Rufus might have got his from Alberta, but they didn't believe it. With the number of stab wounds he had on him, she should have had at least some bloodstains on her white uniform – which she hadn't.

Grave Digger summed it up by saying, "There is no need of thinking about this business until we get more to think about."

"Such as what did the Jew find in this poor domestic worker's furniture of sufficient value to make somebody knock him off," Coffin Ed added.

"And why did Rufus get croaked after he had already completed his part of the deal," Grave Digger threw in.

"Let's find somebody with a roll of fresh money and work back from that," Coffin Ed said, "Our folks will kill one another for damn near anything, but whenever they kill a Jew it's for money."

"Right," Grave Digger said. They were on the second lap of their route when they got the first message of interest. A small-time hoofer from The Celebrity Club on 125th Street told them about a punk who had shown up an hour earlier flashing a roll for the benefit of the chorus girls, trying to score. The hoofer sat in the back seat while the detectives cross-examined him.

"What was his name?" Coffin Ed asked.

"I didn't get it, boss; he's a stranger around here."

"What does he do?"

"I don't know, boss."

"You could tell his pitch from the way he looked."

"I didn't see him, boss. Just heard the girls talking about him. They said he looked like a starker, a real down home mugger. Blowing gage and talking underneath their clothes like as if they were hustlers. They didn't like it."

"What size roll?" Grave Digger asked.

"They didn't count it, boss."

"They saw it."

"Just the edges, boss. He kept it gripped tight in his fist and just flashed the edges."

Grave Digger and Coffin Ed exchanged looks.

"Did he score with any other chippy?" Coffin Ed asked.

"Didn't nobody say, boss. Anyway, he left."

"You're not much good," Coffin said harshly.

"I do the best I can, boss."

"Yeah, if you get caught peddling marijuana to teenagers, you get

57

life under the new Federal law," Grave Digger said. "You know that, don't you?"

"I knows it, boss, but I ain't peddling no weed."

"All right, get out – you stink," Colin Ed said.

The stoolie got from the car as though it had caught on fire.

Grave Digger and Coffin Ed looked at one another.

"What do you make of it?" Grave Digger asked.

"From here it looks like some punk found some stage money and is trying to have a ball on it," Coffin Ed said.

"Yeah, but that's such an old gag for a town like Harlem."

"You know, Digger, Harlem's full of squares," Coffin Ed said.

"Maybe this punk is a square himself," Grave Digger mused. "But we should look into the play just the same – when we get time."

"Right now I want to hear somebody talk about a Jew," Coffin Ed said.

"Right," Grave Digger said, and started up the car.

The next message was a blank. It came from a slap-happy wino whose claim to fame was that once he had fought on the card at Madison Square Garden as a heavyweight. True, he had only been a four-rounder in the prelims and nobody had ever heard of him before or since, but he had been there.

He started out of the Braddock Bar over on Eighth Avenue, saw the dicks' car coming and ducked back in.

"Shall we pass him?" asked Grave Digger, who was driving.

"We haven't got much time," Coffin Ed admitted. "But sometimes out of the mouths of fools comes the solid tip."

Grave Digger smiled to himself

They waited for the wino. He didn't keep them waiting. He approached their car as if he didn't care who saw him, opened the back door without waiting for Coffin Ed and crawled up on the seat. His foul breath filled the car with the smell of stockyards.

"Spit it out and scram," Coffin Ed said brutally. "You are suffocating us."

"You want to know who stuck up that United Cigar store?" the wino asked.

"Who?" Coffin Ed grated.

"Me," the wino said jubilantly, and started laughing like hell.

Coffin Ed was out of the car, big feet planted on the pavement; he had his gun club-fashion in his hand, the back door open; he reached in, grabbed the ex-pug by the collar of his shirt and was yanking him bodily through the door before Grave Digger realized what was happening.

"Don't hurt him, Ed!" Grave Digger cried. "Don't hurt him – he's simple-minded."

Coffin Ed's burn-scarred face was diabolical with fury. But he caught the descending gun butt before it crashed against the wino's skull. He pushed the wino back against the car and slapped him across the mouth.

"You're not funny," he said in a voice so dangerous it sent cold shivers down Grave Digger's spine.

The ex-pug fainted from terror.

Coffin Ed pushed him to one side with his foot.

"Where is your sense of humor, Ed?" Grave Digger asked.

"I haven't got any," Coffin Ed admitted as he holstered his revolver and got back into the car. "They burned it out of me."

Grave Digger started the car, but Coffin Ed halted him by a touch of the arm.

"What do we do with this punk?"

"Leave him there," Grave Digger said. "If he stuck up that cigar store, I'm Cupid."

Coffin Ed grunted.

"It takes all kinds to make the world, Ed," Grave Digger added philosophically.

"Yeah? Some of the funny ones are going to quit work," Coffin Ed said.

They had practically covered their route before they got the last message.

It came from Dummy.

When they saw Dummy duck into the entrance to Sweet Prophet's temple, Grave Digger pulled the battered sedan over the curb and off the street into the exit way beside a chain movie theater. On one side were the double iron doors of the movie house, on the other the brick side wall of the adjoining building.

After a while Dummy showed himself on the sidewalk, walked in that direction – looking on all sides, as was his habit – and suddenly disappeared.

Coffin Ed looked from the darkened car and saw two eyes gleaming beside him in the dark. He opened the back door and Dummy got in.

"What's new?" he asked.

"He can't see in here," Grave Digger said. "Let's take him to the station."

Dummy was squirming about in the back seat, digging out his dirty scratch pad and stub of pencil.

Coffin Ed got into the back seat with him, and Grave Digger backed the car into the street. When they pulled up before the green lights of the precinct station, Dummy scribbled in alarm: *is a pinch?*

Coffin Ed got his face into the light and said, "No pinch, just some questions."

Dummy relaxed and grinned.

They took him to the Pigeon's Nest. He sat on the stool in the spill of white light and imagined he was back in the ring. He looked as happy as a kid with a new toy.

"He'd still fight if they let him," Grave Digger remarked.

Dummy read his lips and nodded vigorously. He jumped to his feet and began shadowboxing, his gaze pinned on the floor, watching his imaginary opponent's feet.

"Sit down," Coffin Ed said, but Dummy wasn't watching his lips, and Coffin Ed had to push him back onto the stool.

Grave Digger brought the two straight backed chairs from the corner desk and they sat facing Dummy in the light.

"Get your paper and pencil out," he said.

Dummy wet the stub in his tongueless mouth and poised the scratch pad on his knee.

"Who killed Rufus?" Grave Digger asked, taking a shot in the dark. He didn't expect an answer, but Dummy was a night bird, and there was always a chance he might know something.

mugger, Dummy wrote without hesitation.

Grave Digger took the pad and passed it to Coffin Ed. They exchanged looks. Grave Digger handed back the pad and asked, "Did you see it?"

Dummy nodded.

"Know him?" Coffin Ed asked.

Dummy shook his head. He drew a circle about his face with his index finger and shook his head again.

"You didn't see his face"

Dummy nodded.

"Tell us what you saw," Grave Digger said.

Dummy wrote: *rufus drove up / mugger braced him in car / pulled him out / put knife on throat/ pushed him toward outhouse / rufus try to run / mugger stab him in back / keep stabbin / rufus down on hands and knees / crawl into the bush / mugger follow / i didn see nobody come out.*

The detectives read the scrawled words in amazement.

"Where were you?" Grave Digger asked.

Dummy reached for the pad and wrote: *i was hidin in bushes.*

60

"Doing what?" Coffin Ed asked, but Grave Digger held up his hand and said, "We'll get back to that. Let's find out what the killer looked like."

Dummy shook his head earnestly.

"All right – you didn't see his face, but you saw his back," Grave Digger said.

Dummy wrote quickly: *i saw his arm risin and fallin with the blade*.

"You saw more than that," Coffin Ed said. "What did he look like? What was he wearing? What size was he?"

Dummy scribbled frantically: *big man built like a heavyweight had on a tan jumper and longbill army cap he was young strong fast all I saw.*

"Was there anyone else in sight?" Grave Digger asked.

i didn see nobody.

As Dummy filled the pages with his answers, Grave Digger tore them from the pad and stuffed them into his pocket.

"What did you do?" he asked.

i ran up the hill i couldn call the cops i didn want tangle with big strong starker and his knife i couldn tell nobody what i saw i wait to tell you.

"You know Sugar Stonewall?" Coffin Ed asked.

Dummy nodded.

"Was it him?"

Dummy shook his head.

"We'd better get the lieutenant in on this," Grave Digger said.

Dummy's mouth flew open, and choking sounds issued from the gruesome cavity.

"It's all right," Grave Digger reassured him. "Take it easy. We have to take a statement."

Beads of sweat came out suddenly on Dummy's scarred, knotty face.

"Who around here talks sign language?" Grave Digger asked his partner.

"The lieutenant, I think," Coffin Ed said. "I've seen him playing with it."

"All right, Dummy, you just sit and take it easy," Grave Digger said, getting to his feet. "We're not going to hold you unless we have to."

Coffin Ed followed, and they went out and locked the door.

Lieutenant Anderson was in command of the night shift. He was a student of dactylology. He took over the questioning of Dummy, translating Dummy's replies for the detectives and a police stenographer, who sat at the desk and recorded the interrogation in shorthand.

Dummy stated that Alberta Wright had visited Cassie in her flat on 112th Street at about ten-thirty o'clock the previous night. She had come alone. He had been absent when she arrived. When he returned home Alberta was sitting at the kitchen table across from Cassie. Cassie was eating watermelon seasoned with black pepper and drinking salted beer.

"Where had you been?" Anderson interrupted to ask.

"I was watching out for my girls," Dummy replied.

"Your girls?"

"He's got two chippy whores," Grave Digger explained. "He's trying to teach them how to hustle. He wants to be a pimp."

Lieutenant Anderson had been on night duty in Harlem for over a year. During that time he had come to know his two ace colored detectives well, and he depended on them. He knew they had their own personal interpretation of law enforcement. Some people they never touched – such as madames of orderly houses of prostitution, operators of orderly gambling games, people connected with the numbers racket, streetwalkers who stayed in their district. But they were rough on criminals of violence and confidence men. And he had always thought they were rough on dope peddlers and pimps, too. So Grave Digger's casual explanation of Dummy's pimping surprised him.

"And you let him go about breaking in young girls to hustle?" he asked.

"If he didn't do that he would do something worse," Grave Digger said. "He would be a mugger or a cat burglar or a stick-up man. He can't talk and he can't hear. He probably could get a job as a porter or a dishwasher; but he won't do that. He has been in the chips, and he figures those jobs are degrading. He used to be one of the greatest welterweights in the business, but the racketeers who owned him sent him to the tank so often he got both his eardrums burst. When he was no longer useful to them, they kicked him out of the profession. Then the do-gooders got hold of him and primed him to spill before the state committee investigating boxing, and the gangsters kidnaped him one night and cut his tongue out. They unloaded him from a car in Foley Square in front of the state building where the investigation was being conducted and it was just luck a patrol car passed in time to get him to hospital to save his life. Since then he has tried his hand at the usual occupations of an ex-pug – writing numbers, gambling, bodyguarding. Some big boxer gave him some money to open a shoe-shine parlor, but he used it to buy a new Cadillac, and the first night he had it he got it smashed up because he couldn't hear the horn of a truck. Now he's trying to pimp. If these chippies don't work for him, they will work for some other pimp. At least he treats them better than most pimps would; he protects them and doesn't beat them up. And when a chippy makes up her mind to be a whore, there is no stopping her. So we let him go. What would you do?"

"God knows," Lieutenant Anderson said. "Let's get back to the story. You live with this woman, Cassie?"

Dummy nodded. "She's my old lady," he said.

"She lets him stay in her house and does what she can to take care of him," Grave Digger explained once more. "But she's just a cook and a liquor-head to boot, so she doesn't have much money. He doesn't make much pimping either, but it keeps him in small change."

"Yeah," the lieutenant said. Then to Dummy, "What did you go home for?"

"To get ten bucks," Dummy confessed. "Tricks weren't walking."

"And Alberta Wright was there when you arrived?"

"Yes, sir," Dummy said.

He told them that Alberta had told Cassie that Rufus had stolen her furniture while she was in a religious trance. She had stopped by to see if she could find out where Rufus lived from Dummy. She and Rufus had worked together for five years after their marriage as a domestic couple – he as the butler-chauffeur and she as the maid-cook. Then he had stolen their savings and had run away with another woman. She hadn't seen him for more than two years, and didn't know where he lived or what name he had taken.

When Dummy came, he had told Alberta the setup. Rufus had been working with the Jew for more than a year in a furniture-stealing racket. Abie had an outlet second-hand furniture store on Third Avenue near 125th Street in Harlem, and another place on Third Avenue in the Bronx, where he kept the hot stuff to cool off. Rufus entered apartments of people who were out of town on visits or business and sold the furnishings to the Jew in the role of proprietor. The Jew was covered; he demanded a statement of ownership from Rufus and gave a signed and witnessed receipt.

Dummy had told Alberta that if she wanted her furniture back, the Jew would return it for what he had paid Rufus, plus twenty per cent handling charges, and ten dollars an hour for its removal and return – no questions asked on either side.

"A slick little racket," Lieutenant Anderson commented.

"I saw her furniture," Grave digger put in. "It wasn't worth that kind of deal."

"That's what Cassie said," Dummy told them. "I told Alberta I would handle it for her, but she just wanted to find Rufus."

"All right, Dummy, quit beating around the bush," Grave Digger said. "What did she have hidden in her furniture that made it worth while to steal?"

"She said it was just mojos and potions and charms," Dummy said. "African and Haitian stuff. Witch doctor bones that had been dried on the equator and special voodoos from the West Indies; hearts' blood from Mexico and dried snake bites from East India. All kinds of magic stuff, she said."

Grave Digger and Coffin Ed looked at one another and then at Lieutenant Anderson. The lieutenant looked nonplused.

"Let's get this straight," the lieutenant said. "She told you she had this stuff hidden in her furniture."

"Yes, sir, that's what she said."

"And you believed it?"

"No, sir, but that's what she said."

Grave Digger chuckled "Can you imagine the Jew going to all that trouble stripping her furniture looking for a handful of mojos?"

"What would she want with mojos if she had just got religion," Coffin Ed said.

"I'm just telling you what she said," Dummy repeated.

"You think it was something else?" Lieutenant Anderson asked the detectives.

"In order to bring the Jew into it, there had to be money," Grave Digger said. "Or else they thought there was money."

"What did you think it was, Dummy?" the lieutenant asked.

"I thought she was just mad at Rufus. He had done stole her money once, and I thought she figured him stealing her furniture was the lick that killed Dick."

"What do you think now?" Coffin Ed asked. "You know the Jew has been killed, too?"

Dummy nodded, "I think it was something else," he admitted.

"What?" Coffin Ed persisted.

"Something she stole," Dummy said. "Some jewelry."

"We can check that soon enough with her employers."

"Maybe she got it from somebody else."

"All right," Anderson said. "You told her where Rufus lived?"

"No, sir," Dummy said. "I told her I would see if I could find out where he lived, and she promised to give me ten dollars if I did."

"And you found out where he lived and told her?"

"No, sir, I knew where he lived," Dummy said. "I left her with Cassie and went to see what I could get out of Rufus. He wasn't at home, and I waited across the street. That's how come I saw him when he drove up."

"You left her with Cassie, and Cassie gave her Rufus's address," the lieutenant said.

"No, sir, Cassie didn't know it," Dummy said. "And she wouldn't have told her nohow."

"We'll soon find out," the lieutenant said. "I'm going to have her brought in."

"It won't do no good," Dummy said. "By now she's stone drunk."

"We'll see," the lieutenant said. He ordered the stenographer to transcribe the notes and have the statement typed, and told the detectives to lock Dummy up until they questioned Cassie.

But Cassie was too drunk to be moved other than in an ambulance, and they figured it best to let her sober up at home.

It was broad daylight by the time the statement was ready for Dummy to sign.

Grave Digger had one last question. "Have you seen Sugar Stonewall?"

Lieutenant Anderson had gone home, and Dummy had to use his pad and pencil to reply. He wrote: *no sir   i aint seen sugar in a week.*

Coffin Ed asked his question. "Who's carrying a fresh roll about town?"

nobody i know of, Dummy wrote.

They let him sign the statement and drove him back to where they had picked him up. Then they drove back to Lenox Avenue, found an all-night greasy spoon, sat on the counter stools and had coffee and doughnuts.

11

"Let's wake up Sweet Prophet," Grave Digger said.

"He ain't going to like it," Coffin Ed said.

"That's for sure," Grave Digger agreed.

Sweet Prophet received the detectives in the sitting room adoining his bedroom on the top floor of the building housing his Temple and reception room.

The housekeeper had opened the curtains and raised the windows looking down on the busy shopping area of 116th Street. Motor sounds and loud voices came in with motor exhaust smell and the stink of hot dirty pavement.

The room had a north light and was furnished like a corner of the lobby of the Paramount Theater. Fat, complacent gold and silver cherubs chased coffee-brown angels about the sunrise-pink wall paper, while the appropriately sky-blue ceiling was filled with more golden stars than in the Milky Way, whirling dizzily about a silver moon containing the vague outline of a face with a startling resemblance to that of Sweet Prophet.

"If this ain't heaven, it will have to do until the real heaven comes along," Coffin Ed remarked.

"Shhh," Grave Digger cautioned. "Here's the Prophet."

Sweet Prophet looked both mad and sleepy. His eyes popped from a scowling countenance. His yellow silk pyjamas, peeping from beneath a dressing gown with candy stripes of red and white, gave the impression of a carnival on the loose. His big feet were encased in bright red Turkish slippers trimmed in gold; and his long kinky white hair was topped with a Fez of matching red with a golden tassel falling from the crown.

He greeted them in a vexed manner. "Gentlemen, I got the best lawyers east of the Mississippi River."

"Okay, throw us out," Grave Digger said.

"Since you're here, sit down, sit down," he said, plumping himself on a high-backed gilded chair that resembled a throne. "We're all colored folks, ain't we? You don't have to stand on ceremony with me. I am a humble man."

The detectives pulled up chairs that put them two feet lower than the Prophet.

"We hate to trouble you at this hour, Prophet," Grave Digger said, "but it's important."

Sweet Prophet folded his hands across his stomach. He was wearing all of his diamond rings, but his long fingernails were encased in protective hard-rubber fingers of matching colors.

It must be hell when he's got to scratch himself, Coffin Ed thought.

"Important!" Sweet Prophet echoed. "More important than a good night's sleep?"

"It's about one of your recent converts," Grave Digger elaborated.

"My God, don't tell me another one has dropped dead – took off – departed, I mean," Sweet Prophet said, searching for the appropriate expression. "That would be the bitter end."

Grave Digger carefully laid his battered hat on the bright green-carpeted floor. He and Coffin Ed had uncovered their heads in deference to the great man.

"No, it's about Alberta Wright," Grave Digger said. "We want to ask you a few questions about her."

"Gentlemen, let the dead rest in peace, I beg you," he said piously. "That poor woman deserves it, as hard as she has worked all of her life."

"That's the point, Prophet," Grave Digger said. "She's not dead."

"What! Not dead!" Sweet Prophet exclaimed in bug-eyed amazement. "Do you mean that woman is still alive? Or has she risen from the dead?"

"Pull yourself together, Prophet," Grave Digger said drily, "She never was dead."

"Good God, man, I saw her die myself," Sweet Prophet snapped.

"She was just unconscious."

"In a trance, you mean." Sweet Prophet fished his yellow silk handkerchief from his candy-striped dressing gown pocket and wiped his dark, sweating brow. "I never thought of that. You startled me."

"And what we're trying to do," Grave Digger went on calmly, "is get her story."

"That woman's story can be told in two lines," Sweet Prophet said. "Born like a fool, and worked like a mule."

67

"That might be so," Grave Digger said. "But we want to know what happened at the baptism."

"God only knows, gentlemen. I blessed the bottle of water – I presume it was water – and she drank it and flopped. I thought she was dead, but you say she went into a trance, and that's all right with me. I'll have to remember it."

"All right, a trance," Grave Digger said. "That is as good as any explanation for the present. How long had she been a follower of yours?"

"Bless my soul, gentlemen, she was not strictly a follower of mine, as you put it. Just a new recruit. I never saw the woman before she came to me yesterday morning to confess her sins and request to be baptized."

"You mean you baptize people without knowing anything about them?" Coffin Ed put in finally.

"Gentlemen, you didn't have to see that woman but once to know everything there was to know about her, like I said before," Sweet Prophet declared. "She was a born kitchen mechanic."

"Okay, be that as it may," Grave Digger said. "What prompted her to get religion all of a sudden?"

"Who knows?" Sweet Prophet said, gesturing with his elongated hands. "Women of that type get religion for ten thousand reasons – some have just murdered their husbands, others have had nightmares."

"She must have given some reason," Grave Digger persisted.

"If she did, I didn't listen," Sweet Prophet said. "Women always lie about the reason they get religion. If I harkened to them, I couldn't last."

"Okay, let's skip it," Grave Digger said. "Just tell me what she might have owned that someone would go to the trouble of stealing."

Sweet Prophet's eyebrows went up an inch, and his eyeballs extended precariously. "You mean to say someone stole something from her?" he asked in an incredulous voice. "Gentlemen, that would be the miracle."

"Her furniture was stolen while she was unconscious, and two people have been killed about it," Grave Digger informed him.

His eyeballs came out so far they seemed on the verge of rolling down his cheeks. "She killed them," he stated more than asked.

"We don't think so," Grave Digger said.

"Look, brothers," Sweet Prophet began, wiping his face with the big yellow handkerchief. "We are more or less in the same business, collaring the sinners. Let us level with each other. Nobody has been killed about that sister's furniture, unless she killed them. I looked on that sister's face and listened to her confession. She has never owned anything in her life that the white folks didn't give her. And they haven't given that sister anything that anybody else would want. She was that kind of woman – is, rather."

"Would you be breaking any kind of vows or such if you told us what sins she confessed to?" Grave Digger asked.

"Nothing worth repeating," Sweet Prophet assured him. "She was just a poor woman living in adultery and working like a dog to pay for it – like any other thousands of poor simple-minded colored women in Harlem. Nothing to make the Lord skin back His ears."

"She had something," Coffin Ed stated.

Sweet Prophet looked at him from his popping eyes. "The only thing that sister had was faith," he said. "And between you and me, gentlemen, her faith were not worth stealing."

"Well, let's try to get some facts," Grave Digger said. "What happened to her after she seemed to drop dead?"

"I never found out," Sweet Prophet confessed. "Until you told me better, I thought the sister at rest with her Maker. Brother Clay's hearse came and took her away, and afterwards the downtown policemen asked me some questions. But one of them got a phone call, and they dropped it without any explanations."

"You didn't make any effort to find out what had happened to her?" Grave Digger asked.

"No, with death the work of Sweet Prophet ends and the Lord takes charge," Sweet Prophet said. "You might ask undertaker Clay."

"We will," Grave Digger said.

He and Coffin Ed stood up.

"Thank you for your cooperation, Prophet," he added. "We hope we haven't disturbed you too much."

"I am always glad to be of service to our colored police," Sweet Prophet declared. "As long as you don't come to arrest me."

"I may as well tell you that Alberta Wright wants to see you, if you haven't already got the message," Coffin Ed said before leaving.

"Don't they all," Sweet Prophet said.

Mr H. Exodus Clay had just come down from his living quarters on the top floor of the old brownstone mansion on 134th Street, where he had his undertaking parlor. He looked more than ever like

69

a body dressed for burial, with his parchment-colored skin still half dead from sleep and his long white dried-out kinky hair freshly combed and brushed.

He received them in his office, the front room that had the light in the window that never went out.

They went straight to the point.

"We're trying to find out what happened to the woman one of your drivers picked up for dead at Sweet Prophet's baptism yesterday," Grave Digger said.

Mr Clay adjusted his pince-nez. "You mean the body that came to life," he said in his dry, impersonal voice. "Just a minute – I will send for the driver."

"It was like this, Mr. Clay," the young man who drove the hearse explained. "They-all sent me to the morgue to get the death certificate. But when I got there the man said I had to bring the body inside so he could look at it before he could give me the certificate, but I couldn't handle it alone and he helped me. We carried it into a big white room and laid it on a long white table, then the man began messing around with a lot of instruments and things and kept on talking about what a fine specimen it was. I asked him if it was dead, and he asked me where I got it from. I told him, and he said it would take him about an hour to finish his examination and for me to go outside and come back in an hour. Then I asked him if it was going to take a whole hour just to find out if it was dead, and he said it wasn't dead but it would take him that much time to find out what was wrong with it. So I figured there wasn't any need of me waiting a whole hour for it if it wasn't dead. So I just came on back here and put the hearse away and wiped it good and clean."

Mr. Clay turned to the detectives and asked, without batting an eye, "Does that answer your question?"

Grave Digger put on his hat, and Coffin Ed did likewise.

"It does indeed," he said.

They went next to the morgue.

The morgue attendant who was on duty Sundays was off on Mondays, and the one on duty didn't know anything about the case.

"You think we ought to rouse him at his house?" Coffin Ed asked.

Grave Digger looked at his watch. "Not this morning. It's already nine o'clock, and my wife has probably begun to worry."

"Mine, too," Coffin Ed said. "So let's call it a day."

"Right," Grave Digger said. "As long as we keep the woman locked up, nothing is going to happen."

12

The three steep flights of stairs led to a long dimly lit hall with eight flanking doors. It was the fourth floor, and that was as high as the stairway went.

Sugar ran to the grimy front window and looked down on the street. Dummy was nowhere in sight. The detectives' car had disappeared, too. He walked slowly back to the other end and joined the girl, who was huddling in the corner. There was something screwy about this business, he was thinking. It was moving too fast. Too much was happening for Alberta's money to have been a secret.

"He lives in there," the girl whispered, pointing toward a warped door showing yellow light about the edges.

Sugar smelt the sharp scent of marijuana coming through the cracks.

"Who?"

"The man I was talking about with all the money."

The door had been fitted with a staple and hasp; it had shrunk so much that the cheap Warder lock was useless.

"If anyone with a lot of money lives in there, he ought to have his head examined," Sugar said absently.

"It ain't his," she said. "He stole it."

"Shut up and let me think," Sugar said.

The only way it made sense was for Dummy to be looking for the money, too, he thought; or how would he know so much about what had happened? And then, as he chewed over that, the whole picture clicked suddenly in his mind.

It all hung on the murder of the Jew. If the Jew hadn't been killed, it might have figured that whoever killed Rufus got the money. But it stood to reason that whoever killed the Jew had already sounded Rufus and was convinced he didn't have it. So he figured the Jew must have it. Because whoever it was must have been someone who had heard Alberta blabbing about her dream at the baptism. All kinds of hustlers hung around Sweet Prophet's activities, hoping some of the Prophet's money would fall off. And then this joker, whoever he was, would have found out where

Alberta lived and beat it over there to burglarize the house. But he, Sugar, had got there first; then, after he had left, Rufus had come; and the Jew had arrived while Rufus was still there and had moved all the furniture. So this joker must have been watching from the street, waiting for a chance to break in, and when he saw the furniture being moved he knew somebody had already got the money. So the logical thing had been to sound Rufus first.

But after he had killed the Jew and hadn't found the money, he figured that Rufus had outsmarted him. So he laid for Rufus.

But by that time Rufus had been warned by the killer's first approach, and he wouldn't be carrying the money around on him. It was ten to one he had hidden it in his own flat, Sugar realized. He had very likely already found it by the time the Jew arrived. Suddenly Sugar understood the reason Rufus decided to sell all the furniture to the Jew – he had already found the money and used that stupid play to cover it up. Rufus must have been laughing at Sugar when they met yesterday afternoon. Yeah, he had been so cute he had gotten himself killed, Sugar thought maliciously.

And now the fact that Dummy had begun to look for it, too, meant that it hadn't been found. Dummy wasn't the kind to waste his efforts on wild-goose chases. It would be just like Dummy to know who killed Rufus and why he was killed – if he hadn't done it himself.

"Come on," he said to the girl.

"Where you going?" she asked.

"What do you care," he said. "You ain't got no other place to go, have you?"

She followed him docilely, relieved at being told what to do. She had never done anything on her own initiative in her life.

He paused in the entrance of the hotel to look up and down the street. No one in sight.

"Where did Dummy go?" he asked.

"How do I know?" she replied stolidly.

"Come on."

She started to walk along with him, but he stopped her.

"You're subject to get arrested for prostitution walking with me," he said. "And I don't want to get picked up, either. So you go ahead, turn down Seventh to a Hundred Twelfth Street and go over to Eighth Avenue. Wait for me on the corner."

She started off without a word. He followed at a distance, but when she turned into the dark side street he kept on down Seventh

Avenue to a once pretentious apartment house in the middle of the block.

Mammy Stormy had a six-room apartment on the top floor, where she gave parties for domestic workers every weekend. They began Saturday night and ended Monday morning. She sold food and drinks, and cut the blackjack game. She called them "house rent" parties because, supposedly, they were for the purpose of paying her rent, but she lived from them.

Back during the depression of the 1930's, everyone who had a house threw these parties to pay their rent. However, most had quit the practice as industrial jobs opened to colored people and the pay for domestic work increased. But Mammy Stormy had kept right on; she hadn't missed one for the past twenty-eight years.

She never left the apartment. She weighed close to four hundred pounds, and she didn't trust elevators and couldn't navigate the stairs. She hadn't worn anything but nightgowns and felt slippers for a decade.

Sugar found her sitting in an ancient armchair in the kitchen, fanning herself with an undertaker's fan. Sweat flowed like a waterfall down her smooth black face. A pot of white beans and chitterlings simmered on the coal-burning stove. Dirty dishes were stacked everywhere; empty bottles were strewn about the floor.

A blackjack game was in progress in the dining room, but the players were just marking time. Other half-drunk, satiated, sleepy people wandered about the other rooms, waiting for daylight and time to go to work.

The smell of food made Sugar's stomach crawl, but he didn't have the price of a dish.

"Dummy sent me," he told Mammy Stormy.

"What do he want now?" she asked.

"His ears hurt him; he wants you to send him some sweet oil," Sugar said.

"Lord, why don't he do something about his ears," she said.

"Do what?" he asked.

That stumped her.

"Look in the bathroom in the medicine cabinet and you'll find the sweet oil," she said. "And tell him don't bring none of his chippy whores into my house."

"I'll tell him," he said.

He found the bottle marked sweet oil, but while he was there he noticed one of her rose-colored nylon nightgowns hanging up to dry. That gave him an idea. He took down the nightgown, took a yellow-orange-and-white-striped bath towel from the rack, rolled them into a bundle and hid them beneath his coat. He left the house by way of the parlor, and didn't see Mammy Stormy again.

It was dawn when he came out onto the street. The girl was waiting on the corner where he had told her to wait. They went toward Manhattan Avenue.

In the middle of the block he stopped in a tenement hallway, removed the label from the bottle of sweet oil and slipped the nightgown over his clothes. Then he tied the towel about his head like a turban. The girl stared at him open-mouthed. She was either too tired or too stupid to laugh.

"What is that for?" she asked.

"Never mind," he told her. "You just keep your mouth shut no matter what I do, and don't laugh."

But the garish ensemble was too much even for Harlem. The crew of a garbage truck making its last round froze in open-mouthed amazement as he approached.

"Great God Almighty, another prophet!" one of them ejaculated.

The girl started to giggle, but Sugar snapped at her. "Shut up!"

They found the janitor of the apartment where Rufus had lived taking in the garbage cans. He put the empty can down and wiped his hand across his eyes. His lips moved as he mumbled something to himself.

He was a big, slow-motioned man with a dark leathery face. Short kinky hair fringed a bald head decorated with a crescent-shaped scar. He wore faded blue denim overalls and a hickory-striped shirt, all neatly washed and pressed. His big misshapen feet were encased in dirt-splotched canvas sneakers. His faded brown eyes gave the impression of a mind that was even slower than his body.

"I'm looking for a gentleman by the name of Mister George Clayborne," Sugar said.

The janitor stared at him stupidly. "What you want him for?" he asked with unconscious rudeness.

"I have an appointment with him," Sugar said.

"Is that so," the janitor said, scratching the scar on his head. "Who is you?"

"I'm a doctor," Sugar said. "This is my daughter and assistant."

The janitor looked at the skinny anemic girl with the cheap torn dress, then back at Sugar's outlandish garb.

"A doctor," he echoed with disbelief. "I ain't never seen a doctor what looks like you, nor an assistant what looks like her, neither."

"I am an African doctor," Sugar said with dignity.

"Oh," the janitor said, looking relieved. "I wondered where you came from wearing them night clothes." He appeared satisfied by the explanation, but he wanted it clarified. "I suppose you is one of them witch doctors."

Sugar drew himself up and gave the impression of being offended. "I am not a witch doctor," he rebuked. "There are other kinds of doctors in Africa besides witch doctors. I am a baby doctor."

"Oh," the janitor said, looking suspicious again. "Mr. Clayborne didn't have no babies."

'I know he doesn't," Sugar said. "That's why he wants me to treat him."

"I don't get that," the janitor said frankly. "You is a baby doctor and a man wants you to treat him who ain't got no babies."

"I treat people so they can get babies," Sugar explained patiently. "If a man has lost his potency and can't make any babies, I give him massages with my magic oil. One massage is enough to start him going." Reaching down through the décolleté of the nightgown, he extracted the bottle of sweet oil from his jacket pocket.

"You got on regular clothes underneath," the janitor observed, his diminishing suspicions increasing again.

"Of course I have on regular clothes," Sugar said. "This gown is my doctor's uniform."

"Oh," the janitor said. That appeared to satisfy him.

"This oil," Sugar went on to explain, "is made from the fat of the tails of bull kangaroos mixed with the essence of the productive organs of lions. It will make you hop like a kangaroo and roar like a lion. After three massages any man of any age will become a father."

The janitor's eyes popped with interest and amazement.

Sugar pinned a stare on him. "Are you a father?" he demanded.

"I got grown children," the janitor stammered guiltily. "I'm sixty-four years old. But my wife, she got two young kids by her first husband."

"You are an old man," Sugar said, tapping him on the chest with his forefinger to drive home the point. "You got a young wife. You are in trouble mister."

"You telling me, doctor," the janitor said. "You don't know what trouble is."

Sugar poked him in the ribs. "After you have had three massages with this magic oil, your troubles will be over. She won't look at another man. You will have her eating out of your hand."

The janitor giggled gleefully. "He he. Wouldn't that be something?"

Sugar looked sympathetic but said regretfully, "I'm afraid I won't have time for you this morning, as much as I would like to help you."

"Oh," the janitor said, wilting disappointedly.

"I have to treat Mr. Clayborne, and I have other patients," Sugar explained.

"You don't have to worry about Mr. Clayborne," the janitor said with rising spirits. "He's dead."

"Dead!" Sugar exclaimed in amazement. "When did he die? How did it happen? I talked to him just yesterday, and he looked in fine health, other than he couldn't make babies."

"He was stabbed to death last night," the janitor informed him. "Right over there in them bushes," he added, pointing toward the park.

Sugar glanced at the clump of bushes in the park and shuddered. "It's a pity," he said. "Such a fine man. He would have made a good father." Sighing, he added, "Well, in that case I will take you in his place."

The janitor hesitated. "The only thing is I got to get my morning chores done first, and that takes some time. If you don't mind waiting, I will pay you –"

Sugar cut him off with an impatient gesture. "I do not charge for my services," he said with asperity. "My patients give me whatever they can afford. But I can not give you a treatment later on. This magic only works during the first hour of the day, and tomorrow I am going on to Philadelphia." He turned to the girl and said, "Come on, Mamba, we can't keep our other patients waiting."

"Wait a minute, doctor," the janitor begged. "I'll just leave those chores if you'll give me a treatment."

Sugar hesitated with reluctance. "Well," he finally conceded. "If there is no delay."

"Oh, there won't be no delay," the janitor promised eagerly. "If you-all will just follow me."

He led them along the alley beside the building and through a side doorway into a whitewashed basement corridor. Overhead were asbestos-covered steam pipes, and on each side were freshly painted green doors to the various basement rooms.

Before one of the doors he said, "Can you-all wait here a minute, doctor, while I get the keys? I don't want my wife to know about it."

He went around a corner, and they heard him opening the door to his living quarters. A woman's sleepy voice said crossly, "Is you just got to make so much noise and wake up the children?" They heard a door close softly, and he reappeared with a brass ring the size of a knitting hoop, containing all the master keys.

He unlocked the door, and they entered a storeroom filled with trunks, packing cases and a few odd items of furniture belonging to the tenants.

"Make a place to lie down," Sugar directed.

The janitor put two steamer trunks end to end and dusted them off.

"Remove your overalls and underwear," Sugar directed.

"You mean take them off?" the janitor asked.

"How do you expect me to massage you with them on?" Sugar asked.

The janitor looked embarrassed. "With her here?"

"She's seen a lot of bare backsides," Sugar said.

Giggling with embarrassment, the janitor slipped off the shoulder braces of his overalls and let them fall to his ankles. He was wearing boxer-type shorts with red roses on a purple background. He let these fall to his ankles also, keeping his back turned to the girl; then he lay on his stomach across the trunks.

The girl watched these proceedings in a stolid, unsmiling, unblinking amazement.

Sugar poured oil on the leathery skin and began massaging. He mumbled sounds, which the janitor believed to be magic words of an African language.

The janitor had placed the key ring on the dusty top of a nearby dressing table.

After a few minutes, Sugar said, "My assistant will continue while I go wash my hands. Where is there a wash basin I can use?"

"Hand me my keys, doc," the janitor said without moving. He separated one and gave the ring back to Sugar. "This is for the boiler room; it's the third door to the right. You'll find everything you want there."

Sugar took the keys and motioned for the girl to begin massaging the janitor's back. She took over and began rubbing stolidly back and forth like a Spanish peasant washing clothes on a stone slab.

Sugar left the room. He was grateful to the janitor for giving him the keys; otherwise he would have had to take them. He found the door to the boiler room, unlocked it and entered. He stayed long enough to take off the nightgown and towel and put them in the furnace. Then he found his way up to the ground floor and continued up to the second floor by means of the front stairs. He took his time trying the various keys until he found one that unlocked the door to the apartment formerly occupied by Rufus. The door opened on a small hallway that connected the two front rooms and a bathroom to one side. Rufus had done well by himself, Sugar thought.

He went through the sitting room, opened the front window and looked up and down the street. A few early risers were up and about; but it didn't take long to catch a moment when the street was clear. He tossed the keys so that they fell directly in front of the entrance. Then he closed the window and drew the curtains.

He wondered how long it would take the janitor to discover he'd been tricked. As for the girl, if no one stopped her she would keep on rubbing until the skin came off.

He began to search.

13

The keys were lying in the street.

It's a trap, Dummy thought automatically. Nobody could go to a joint looking for some way to get in and find the keys lying at his feet. Life wasn't that easy.

But if the police thought he would fall into their trap, they didn't know Dummy. He looked quickly up and down the street, trying to spot the stake-out. But he didn't see anyone who looked like a dick. Two women who couldn't be anything but housemaids were trudging toward the bus-stop; a late worker was hurrying toward the subway kiosk on 110th Street.

Dummy didn't believe that Grave Digger and Coffin Ed would be that crude; so it must be the Homicide men playing around. Well, he would play around, too.

He kept on walking like an ordinary man on his way down the street, going about his business. He didn't see the keys. It was by the merest accident that his foot kicked the ring. He picked them up and went looking for the janitor like an honest man, holding them openly in his hand. He looked into the vestibule, then came back to the sidewalk. He went over and peered down the alleyway beside the building. He came back and stood in the vestibule. There was a button beside the mail boxes marked *Super*, but he didn't see it. If he had, he would have rung it, and, when someone answered it, he would have given them the keys.

He was making up the story as he went along, and making himself believe it.

He tiptoed up the stairs, walking on the balls of his feet. Every nerve in his body was alert. His hands hung free and his shoulders were loose, ready to throw a punch with either hand from any angle. He didn't find the janitor on the second floor as he expected. Someone – he supposed it was one of the tenants on his way to work – had told him he had seen the janitor on the second floor cleaning out the apartment of the man who had been killed the night before.

But the door to that apartment was closed. He didn't try the knob. Instead, he rang the bell.

Sugar was inside of the hall closet to the left of the entrance when the bell rang. It sounded right over his head. He was going through the pockets of Rufus's clothes. He jumped so violently he struck his head against the shelf above the clothes rack. Luckily, it didn't make much of a sound, but it raised a knot. After that he was afraid to move. He held his breath, while ice-cold chills ran up and down his spine. He strained his ears, trying to catch the sound of movement outside, meanwhile keeping his nerves braced against another ring. But the bell didn't ring any more, and for a time he didn't hear a sound.

Dummy had taken out his scratch pad and pencil. He wrote, *janitor I found your keys,* on a page and tore it from the pad.

Sugar heard the sound of paper tearing.. It shattered his nerves more than a hammering on the door would have done. He couldn't figure it out. Then he saw the edge of a piece of paper pushed underneath the door. There was little more than an inch of the paper showing and nothing was written on that part. He stared at it as though it were a time bomb. Hackles rose on the back of his neck. What did it mean?

Dummy had inserted the paper so that the greater part still remained outside. Then he tiptoed to the staircase and stood back out of sight from the door, only the edge of his face showing as he peeped around the corner to see if anyone would draw the paper inside.

Sugar felt instinctively that it was a trap. But he couldn't be sure. It might be a warning. No, that was out; it couldn't be a warning – not for himself, at any rate. But it might be a message to Rufus by someone who didn't know yet that Rufus was dead. It might have something to do with the money; it might be the key to the whole thing.

He got down on his hands and knees and tried to look underneath the door. He couldn't see anything. He stared at the strip of paper. There must be something written on the part he couldn't see, he thought. But he was afraid to touch it. The odds were too great that it might be a trap. Someone was trying to find out if anyone was in the flat. If it were the police, they would have simply come on in. They would not have rung the bell. The only person who would set that kind of trap was the person who had killed Rufus, he concluded.

He heard a key being inserted in the lock.

Dummy had satisfied himself that there was no one within the flat. If the police had a stake-out, he must be in another apartment.

80

Dummy decided he'd have to risk it. There was always the possibility that the janitor had dropped his ring of keys. And if the police did catch him, he could claim that he found the keys in the door.

Sugar scuttled away from the door, crawling on all fours like a frightened crab. He needed a weapon – a good solid club. The killer was a knife-man, and Sugar's only hope was to knock him out before he got a chance to use it.

He had been through the sitting room and bedroom before, and he didn't remember having seen anything sufficiently substantial. So he made for the kitchen. His first choice was the kitchen stool, but then he noticed a heavy iron skillet with a grip handle that was just the thing.

He snatched it from the hook and rushed back to the door, stationing himself on the opening side so he'd be behind the door when the intruder entered.

The fourth key worked. Dummy had the door open and the key extracted and was stepping into the room, holding the key ring in his right hand, when his sixth sense sounded the alarm. He ducked backwards with the automatic instinct of the ring, and the heavy iron skillet passed by his head so close he felt the backwash. He circled out of the ducking motion like a piston on a cam shaft and came back with a shoulder smash against the door that knocked Sugar off his feet. Dummy was through the door, and had kicked it shut behind him, while Sugar was still clawing the air. It was over in a second. He led with a left to the ribs and crossed a right to Sugar's solar plexus. Sugar sat on the floor, and the lights dancing before his eyes kept him from breathing.

Dummy was surprised to find out it was Sugar. He wondered how much Sugar knew. Alberta had given him the impression that Sugar didn't know about the money; or why hadn't she asked Sugar to find out where Rufus lived instead of coming to him? But it looked now as though Sugar knew as much as he did – which wasn't much of anything, he admitted to himself. In fact, Sugar might know more. His eyes narrowed with suspicion.

Sugar kept gasping until his vision returned. He saw Dummy standing over him.

"It was you," he gasped.

Dummy continued to stare at him.

Sugar remained in his sitting position on the floor.

"You killed him," he said gaspingly.

Dummy took out his stub of pencil and scratch pad and wrote: *I saw you kill him but I didn't tell.*

Sugar read it and got to his feet. He was scared. "Look here, man, if you're thinking of trying to frame me, I can prove I didn't do it. How about you?"

Dummy showed him a tongueless grin and wrote the question: *what you doin here?*

"What are you doing here yourself?" Sugar countered.

Dummy wrote: *quit playin dumb   i am lookin for the money like you is.*

"It's Alberta's money," Sugar said. "I'm going to see that she gets it back."

Dummy wrote: *not if i find it first.*

"All right, we'll go halvers," Sugar bargained.

Dummy wrote: *just if we find it in here   outside dont count.*

Sugar nodded. There would be time enough to work out what to do after they found it. The main thing was to keep a close watch and protect himself, because if Dummy had killed Rufus, he wouldn't hesitate about killing him, too.

Dummy wrote: *we search together.*

Sugar nodded. "That's the best way," he agreed.

It was not a difficult place to search. The two rooms and kitchen had been furnished from Blumstein's department store on 125th Street. The sitting room furniture was of modernistic oak veneer, was known as the King Cole suite, and had been manufactured in the Bronx. In the bedroom was a Deluxe bridal suite in bland maple from Grand Rapids, Michigan. The television set bore the stamp of one of the big Jersey City dealers, who advertised over the local radios that he would deliver, install and have working, within one hour of receiving an order by telephone, any size television set to any of New York City's five boroughs at any time of the day or night.

Before starting, Sugar had gone into the kitchen for a glass of water. Dummy had followed quickly, but not before Sugar had snatched the plastic pepper shaker from the kitchen table and slipped it into his side pants pocket. He managed to unscrew the top while they went over the furnishings and through all of the various drawers.

Neither let the other get out of sight. Chiefly, they watched one another's hands. Every now and then they stared at each other with secret speculation. It was Sugar's intention, if Dummy found the money, to dash the pepper into his eyes, snatch the money and run. Dummy's plan was not so subtle; he merely intended to knock Sugar unconscious and walk out with the money, leaving him there.

82

But they didn't find anything except the worldly possessions of Rufus Wright, which weren't worth talking about.

Dummy wrote: *somebody beat us to it.*

"It didn't have to be here," Sugar said.

Dummy wrote: *where else.*

Sugar shook his head. He wasn't giving Dummy any leads.

Before leaving, they went to the window to case the street. There was the customary array of downtown porters and domestic workers on their way to work. They didn't spot anyone who looked like a detective. But while they were watching they saw the girl come from the alleyway, carrying a pair of overall pants, and start highballing in the direction of 114th Street. A moment later the janitor appeared in his hickory-striped shirt and flowered shorts and took out after her. They disappeared around the corner.

Dummy looked at Sugar and wrote the question, *you bring my girl here?"*

Sugar nodded, without offering any further explanations.

Dummy didn't ask for any; he wrote: *you owe me.*

"I'll pay you," Sugar said, thinking it was no more than right. "I ain't got it now, but I'll pay you later."

They shook hands to seal the agreement.

Sugar left first, whistling nonchalantly as he walked rapidly in the direction of 110th Street.

Dummy remained long enough to give the flat another quick going over; then he paused for a moment in the downstairs vestibule to search the street with his roving gaze. Satisfied, he placed the ring of keys on the sidewalk where he had found them and headed in the opposite direction. He had both hands in his pockets, and he shuffled along looking as innocent as a five-year-old English bulldog who had just killed the neighbor's pedigreed cat.

14

"What time is it?" the bus driver asked the roving checker at the bus stop at 111th Street.

The checker consulted his watch. "Seventeen minutes and thirteen seconds past seven o'clock," he said.

The driver synchronized his watch and put the bus in gear.

Sugar had been standing with the people waiting for the bus, but he hadn't got on board. He had been watching to see Dummy leave the building up the street. He had seen him come out, place the keys back on the sidewalk and walk off, but a moment later a woman jostled him, and, when he got the street in focus again, Dummy had vanished. However, he was satisfied that Dummy had gone about his business.

He hastened back toward the house, but a woman tenant on her way to work had beaten him to the keys. She was ringing the super's bell when he arrived.

Dummy watched him from the doorway up the street where he had ducked. He grinned to himself. He figured that Sugar had doubled back to search the flat again; perhaps Sugar had found a likely hiding place and had saved it for a private search. But Dummy was satisfied that the money wasn't there.

He waited until Sugar re-entered the building. Then he kept on his way, this time without hesitating or looking back.

Sugar made as if to pass the woman, then stopped and looked inquiringly at the keys.

"You want to return the super's keys?" he asked.

"I found them in the street," she said defensively.

"He must have dropped them," Sugar said. "I'm just going downstairs. I'll take them to him."

The woman looked at him suspiciously, but she was late and didn't have time to argue. She handed him the ring grudgingly, saying, "I hope I'm doing right; I hope you ain't no burglar." He was about to protest, but she salved her conscience by adding, "Anyway, I have rung the bell."

Without replying, Sugar hastened through the basement doorway and descended the stairs. He hadn't seen the janitor return, but it was a risky business.

He found the janitor's wife standing in the open door to their quarters, looking up and down the corridor. She was what he had expected, a loose, ripe, high-yellow woman with cowlike eyes and a petulant expression. Smooth fat arms and mounts of cream-colored flesh showed above the décolleté blue rayon nightgown, and black hair hung in long greasy curls about her shoulders.

When she saw it was a man she became coy, more from habit than desire, and asked in a simpering voice, "Did you ring my bell?"

"Yes, ma'am," he said politely, letting his gaze rove approvingly over her padded figure. "I found these keys on the sidewalk out front."

Her expression changed instantly to one of suspicion. "Where's he at?"

"The last I saw of him he was chasing some young girl," Sugar said.

The next instant her face darkened with an evil look. "I'll fix him," she threatened. "Around here chippy-chasing at this hour of the morning."

"Can I come in?" Sugar asked. "I want to ask you some questions."

"Come right on," she said, merely turning her body to let him pass.

She took up most of the doorway, and in passing he rubbed against her body. It was a pleasure.

At seven-forty-four, Alberta was taken by a matron from the cell that she occupied with two other colored women into the small reception room, where lawyers interviewed their clients and detectives re-examined suspects.

She still wore the maid's uniform, but now it was gray all over, and streaked with black. She had removed the bathing cap, and her straightened hair stuck out in all directions. She looked bone-tired, and her expression was sullen.

The shyster waiting for her knew his way around. He had a degree in law from a colored university in Washington, D.C., and a license to practice in New York State. Most of his business was making bail for prostitutes and racketeers and pleading them guilty if the fine was right. His youthful, grinning black face inspired confidence in most people, but it had the opposite effect on Alberta.

"Slick sent me," he said.

"Who is you?" she asked.

"I'm his lawyer," he said.

"What he want?" she asked.

"He said if you will tell him where it is and go halvers, he will get you out when he gets it," he said.

"I wouldn't be surprised but what he ain't already got it himself," she said.

"What would he want to make a deal for if he already had it?" he asked.

"Because if he's got it, he's got two murder charges to go along with it," she said.

"That's just the point," he said. "He ain't got it, and you got the two murder charges instead."

"How can he get me out?" she asked.

"He's got somebody tapped for the killings," he said.

"What killing?" she asked.

"Both of them," he said.

"Then he knows who done them," she said.

"I didn't say that," he denied. "I said he can give somebody to the police to satisfy them so they will let you go."

"I don't want him to do that if the person he's going to accuse ain't guilty," she said.

"All right then, let's say the person is guilty. Does that satisfy you?" he asked.

"Is it somebody I know?" she asked.

He hesitated. "He don't know if it's anybody you know or not. He don't know who you know. It's not your man, if that's what you want to know," he said.

"All right – I'll give him half when I get out if he tells the police who did it," she bargained slyly.

"You've got to tell him where it is first," he said.

"You've got to give me time to think," she said, stalling.

He looked at his watch. "Listen, woman, you ain't got no time to think," he said. "I got to be out of here by eight o'clock, and I'm not coming back, and your case is coming up at ten o'clock."

"You go back and tell Slick he had better watch himself," she said. "God is going to strike him dead like He done those other two."

He jumped up in exasperation. "You are a religious fanatic, woman," he charged. "I don't want to talk to you any more. You're crazy."

"He's the crazy one," she said, "if he thinks I'm going to split half with him because I'm here in jail for something I ain't never done."

He snatched up his cream-colored straw hat with the fancy red-and-blue polka dot band and left.

The matron took her back to her cell.

At eight-three, Sugar reappeared in front of the house by way of the main entrance just as the janitor was turning into the alleyway beside the house. They saw each other at the same instant. Sugar noticed that the janitor was again decently clad in his overalls. Then he took off, running.

The janitor turned and gave chase.

After they had run about half a block, the janitor called, "Hey, doc! Hey, doc!" They ran another half block and the janitor shouted again, "It worked, doc! It worked!"

Sugar couldn't figure that out. If the janitor hadn't discovered he had been tricked, then why had he chased the girl? That took some deep figuring. But he didn't have the time for it. And what was more, he wasn't taking any chances on stopping and demanding an explanation. He turned the corner into 112th Street running on the edges of his soles and ducked into the first tenement doorway. He hid on the stairs, looking around the banister, and saw the janitor run past. But he didn't leave until he saw the janitor come walking back.

Then he slipped from the building and kept on over to Eighth Avenue, went up to 117th Street, turned back toward Manhattan Avenue and entered a building in the middle of the block. It was a walk-up in fairly good repair; the tiled floors were clean, and the walls were painted.

He walked up to the third-floor front and pushed a buzzer beside a bright red lacquered door. A respectable-looking buxom brown-skinned woman wearing gold-rimmed glasses opened the door onto a chain and asked through the crack, "Who you want to see?"

"Mabel," he said.

The woman smoothed her gray-streaked hair and looked at him appraisingly.

"She ain't in," she decided to say.

"When will she be in?" he asked.

"It's hard to tell," she said. "Who shall I tell her called?"

"She don't know me," he said. "Just tell her I've come from Rufus and I'll be back."

"You say you come from Rufus!" she echoed. Her eyes popped

behind the glittering spectacles. "And you say you is coming back. Naw, you ain't, neither!" she concluded, and slammed the door in his face.

"I shouldn't have told her that," he admitted to himself. "She must know that Rufus is dead."

It was eight-twenty-nine.

"Well, well," Sergeant Ratigan from Homicide said. "You are the woman who started all this business. And it looks from here as if you finished it off, too."

Alberta remained silent and sullen.

He was questioning her in the same room where the shyster had propositioned her less than an hour previously.

"Tell me," he said. "Just between us friends, why were you playing dead?"

"I wasn't playing dead," she denied stolidly.

He crossed his legs and strapped his hands about one of his bony knees. "What were you doing then?" he asked. "Playing a joke?"

"I don't know what I was doing," she said.

"Just so," he said, and took time out to reread the long report turned in by Grave Digger and Coffin Ed.

"Everyone is convinced you are not guilty, it seems," he said on finishing. He showed her the front rows of his tobacco-stained teeth in what he thought was a sympathetic grin, inviting confidence. "Now! All you have to do is tell me who did it and you can go."

"Go home?" she asked.

"Right," he said.

"I don't know who did it, and that's the God's truth," she said.

He sighed and took a cheap cigar from his pocket. He cut the cellophane band with a small penknife, snipped off the end of the cigar and punctured it with the point of the knife. He lit it with a paper match, spinning it between thumb and forefinger until it was burning evenly.

"All right, Alberta, you can't get away with playing stupid," he said. "Now I want you to tell me what happened from the time you drank the water at the baptism until you were arrested with the bloodstained knife."

"The last thing I remember was feeling the Spirit creeping all through me after I had drunk the water Sweet Prophet blessed and then seeing visions –"

"What kind of visions?" he interrupted with quickened interest.

"Visions of heaven," she said.

88

His interest faded.

"The air looked like it was full of stars and bubbles, and then it seemed like I fell down and all around me was the faces of angels," she went on.

"What kind of angels?"

"Colored angels. They looked just like ordinary people, but I knew they were angels. I thought I was dying and going straight to heaven. I was that happy!" she stated.

"The prophet said you had a religious trance," he informed her. "Do you believe that?"

"He's a prophet – he ought to know," she said. Then suddenly she was struck by the realization of what he had said. "Oh, you mean a *religious trance!*" The weariness and sullenness were wiped from her face, and her smooth, dark, immature features lit with ecstasy. "A religious trance," she echoed wonderingly. "Me, Alberta Peavine Wright. I had myself a religious trance. What do you know about that!"

"All I know about it is what I'm told," he said drily, and then suddenly asked, "What did the water taste like?"

"Taste like?" she repeated. "It tasted just like holy water."

"What does holy water taste like? I have never tasted any."

"It tastes just like water what has been made holy," she said. "What do you want me to say?"

"I just want you to say what is true."

"Well, that is true."

"That you drank the water and went into a religious trance?"

"Yassuh." Not the slightest hint of a doubt showed in her face. "Ain't I the lucky one," she exulted. "I'm going to write home and tell Ma so she can tell Reverend Tree, who is always bellyaching about us living in sin up here in Harlem."

"All right, come down to Earth and let the Lord rest for a moment," he said peevishly. "You were taken to the morgue by a mistake, and you were still there when you regained consciousness. You know all about that?"

"Yassuh."

"You were released from the morgue at four-twenty-six o'clock – so the record states. What did you do?"

"I went home," she said.

"Just that?" he persisted.

"Well, I didn't know then that I had had a religious trance," she elaborated. "The man in the morgue said I had fainted probably from a sunstroke or else being too excited. So I just caught a bus and

89

went home. When I found my furniture had been stolen, I went downstairs and asked Miz Teabone had she seen anybody suspicious about the house. She lives on the first floor and has a window on the street, and she sees nearmost everything that happens around there –"

"I don't doubt it," he muttered.

"She told me what she had seen, and I knew it was some of Rufus's doings," she continued.

He pounced on her. "How did you know it was Rufus?"

"How did I know it were him?" she repeated. "For one thing she described him, and I knew right away it was him because wouldn't anybody else be mean enough to me to steal my furniture. He's always stealing something from me," she added.

"So you started searching for Rufus. With a knife," he said.

"Nawsuh, that ain't so," she said. "I first started looking for Sugar Stonewall. I hadn't seen him since just before it happened and –"

"Just before what happened?" he cut in.

"My religious trance," she replied doggedly. "I didn't know where he had gone or what had happened to him, and I needed him to help me look for Rufus, so I started looking for him first."

He looked at the report again and conjectured. "You must have gotten home at about five o'clock."

"Nawsuh, not that soon. It were Sunday and the buses were slow, and it was nearer six o'clock when I got home. And then, after I found my furniture gone, it took me some time to get myself together. I had just got religion, and I didn't want to go and lose it the first thing. Then it must have taken me an hour to talk to Miz Teabone – she asked that many questions. So it must have been seven-thirty or eight o'clock when I started looking for Sugar."

"And it was around ten-thirty when you wound up at Cassie's. You spent three hours looking for Sugar."

"Yassuh. It took every bit of that long. I went everywhere I thought he might be at."

"Where would all those places be?"

"Oh, around and about," she said. "If you don't know Harlem, it wouldn't be no use of telling you."

"This is quite different from what you told before," he pointed out.

"Yassuh, I'm telling the truth now," she said.

"All right, when did you leave Cassie's?" he asked.

"I don't know exactly. I left there right after Dummy left. I happened to remember that Rufus was on the H."

"Heroin?"

"Yassuh. And I asked Cassie where people bought that stuff. She told me there was a place in a house on 110th Street called Esther's, and I went there and sat on a bench in the park across the street where I could watch the door. I figured that after he had got the money for my furniture he would be going there sooner or later to buy some dope. And after that it were just like I said – I saw the patrol car pass and turn into Manhattan Avenue, and I had a premonition."

"You needn't go into that again," he said. "It is all written down here."

"It is?" she asked in surprise.

"Yes, everything you said has been taken down," he told her. "Now, tell me, just exactly what were these people looking for?" he asked. "Had you come by some money recently?"

"Nawsuh," she denied stolidly.

"Jewelry?"

"Nawsuh."

"You mean to sit there and tell me that these two smart people went to all that trouble and got themselves killed just to get hold of your worn out furniture?"

"It weren't worn out," she denied.

"Worn out or not," he snapped. "Do you want me to believe that was all they were after?"

"It looks like it," she replied evasively.

"It doesn't look like it to me," he said.

"Unless they had some other reasons I didn't know nothing about," she added.

"Listen, Alberta, if you play square with me, I will play square with you," he promised.

"Yassuh," she said noncommittally.

"What did you have?"

"I done told you," she said. "I didn't have nothing but my furniture."

"All right," he said wearily. "That's your story."

She didn't say anything.

"Who were Rufus's friends?" he asked, trying another tactic.

"I didn't know them," she said.

"Who was his girl friend? You would know that. He was your husband. You would certainly be curious enough to know who his girl friend was."

"Nawsuh. I didn't care nothing about him nor his girl friend, nor about anything he did – long as he left me alone," she said.

"He stole your savings and ran away with a woman and you don't know who she is," he said incredulously.

"Nawsuh, I never knew," she said.

"And you didn't do anything about it," he said sarcastically.

"Oh, I would have cut his throat at the time, if I could have found him," she confessed. "But he left town so I couldn't find him and I got over it. That was what first turned me to Jesus."

"That I believe," he said. "Now this is the last time I am going to ask you," he went on. "What did you have that was so valuable that two smart men got killed for stealing it?"

"They must have got killed for something else," she said doggedly.

He wiped his face with the palm of his hand. "Be reasonable, Alberta," he pleaded with her. "We have got to establish the motive."

"I done told you all I know," she maintained stubbornly.

"Well, since you won't tell me, you are going to have to tell the Grand Jury," he said, getting to his feet.

15

At nine-thirteen o'clock Dummy was sitting on a stool behind a dilapidated wooden pushcart, watching the entrance of the hotel on 116th Street across from Sweet Prophet's Temple Of Wonderful Prayer.

His friend, the pushcart proprietor, was carefully quartering watermelons and arranging the quarters on cracked ice in the bed of the pushcart, beneath the strip of faded tan canvas that would protect them from the sun.

Dummy saw the young man pause in the hotel entrance beneath the faded sign and case the street in both directions. But the young man did not see Dummy.

This young man was lucky that he was not wearing a tan jumper and a long-billed army cap, because all young men of his size and age wearing tan jumpers and long-billed army caps were being picked up by the police that morning.

Instead the young man was wearing a heavy tweed jacket with thick shoulder pads, a wide-brimmed beaver hat pulled low over his forehead and skintight mustard-colored corduroy pants tucked into black and white cowboy boots.

Dummy's little prostitute could have identified him as the one who had cheated her much earlier that morning, but she was not there.

Two dark buxom housewives in cotton shifts, carrying shopping bags loaded with assorted groceries, passed the hotel entrance. The young man raised his beaver hat and grinned at them with a suddenness that was startling. The women stiffened with offended dignity, passed him without a word and then, a few paces farther on, looked at one another and giggled.

Dummy knew instantly that the young man was sky high on marijuana. He grinned to himself. That was going to make it easy.

The young man stepped to the sidewalk and turned in the direction of Seventh Avenue. Dummy got from his stool and followed at about a ten-yard distance. The pushcart proprietor continued to fiddle with his watermelon display without giving him a glance.

93

The young man walked with an exaggerated swagger, tipping his beaver hat indiscriminately to all the women he passed. Beneath the padded coat his shoulders looked as wide as a team of yoked oxen.

Dummy followed in the shuffling, half-crouching gait of a prize fighter stalking his opponent. He looked constantly to both sides and over his shoulder, using his eyes in place of ears.

The young man joined the people waiting for the bus around the corner. He puffed his cigarette rapidly, made erratic, meaningless gestures and stared into the women's faces.

Dummy loitered in front of a jewelry store next to the corner. The window was filled with watches, atop price tags giving the credit terms. He saw the reflection of the bus when it approached 116th Street.

It was a green Fifth Avenue bus, a Number Two. It came up Fifth Avenue to the north end of Central Park, turned over to Seventh Avenue, and passed through the middle of Harlem.

Dummy waited until it had almost finished loading, then dashed around the corner and hopped aboard.

The young man had stayed up front. Dummy took a seat in the back and looked out of the window.

The Theresa Hotel Grill looked busy, but the hotel entrance was dead; not even the doorman was on duty, and the sports who held up the walls later in the day had not yet awakened. The big two-faced clock on the opposite corner in front of the credit jeweler's said six minutes after nine.

Along the way the RKO movie theater was closed, the churches were closed, the bars were closed, the pool rooms were closed, the undertakers were closed. Hotel entrances looked dead; a trickle of shoppers patronized the various food stores. Only the greasy spoons were doing good business.

Across 145th Street, Seventh Avenue passed between two housing developments, the Rockefeller-built Dunbar Apartments and the slum clearance Federal Housing Project. They looked dead, too.

At 155th Street the bus turned west onto the end of the bridge over the Harlem River and passed high above one of Father Divine's Heavens on the roof of which, in giant white letters, was the word *peace*. Then it turned north into the winding strip of Edgecombe Drive, overlooking the flats along the river bank.

Dummy heard the bell ring, and, as the bus slowed down for the stop at 157th Street, he saw the young man go down the stairs. He let the young man alight; then, just before the door closed, he jumped up to follow as though he'd forgotten his stop. The young man recognized him; Dummy was known to everyone in the Harlem underworld.

But Dummy didn't give the young man a glance. He waited for the bus to drive on and cut across the street.

Only one side of the Drive was built up; the other was a steep rocky park descending to the flats, on which were built the Polo Grounds and a new housing development.

Without hesitating, Dummy entered the ornate lobby of the Roger Morris Apartment House, better known as 555. In its day it had been a very pretentious apartment dwelling for upper income whites, but now it was occupied for the most part by successful colored racketeers, jazz musicians, madames and current prize fighters.

He knew that, when the young man had come this far, he was coming here. And he knew there would be nothing to arouse the young man's suspicions in his coming here, too. He stood in the hall, talking in sign language to the dumb porter, whose hero he was. The young man came in and saw them talking. His face burst into its sudden moronic grin, and he made some eccentric gestures with his hands as though to join in the conversation. The two mutes ignored him.

He went back to the elevators and went upstairs.

Dummy and the porter talked about prize fighting. The porter leaned on his mop and let the water stand on the floor. A young woman, passing as a model or a showgirl, came from the elevator and had to walk through the dirty soapy water in her fragile pink shoes. She complained with shocking vulgarity, and the porter told her with gestures what she could do. Dummy went on saying that with a few weeks training he'd be in shape to take on the Cuban Kid.

The young man came down accompanied by a middle-aged man equally as tall but slimmer, with a pale tan ascetic-looking face. He was dressed in a tropical worsted suit of slate blue, black and white shoes, a dull ivory-colored shirt and a tie and matching display handkerchief the color of tarnished silver.

"Who are they?" Dummy asked his friend.

"The slick is a payoff man for the Tia Juana numbers house," the porter said. "I haven't seen the starker before." Then he added, "The slick is called Slick."

With his hands Dummy said, "I'll be hearing you," and moved off.

Outside, Slick and the starker separated. Slick got into an olive

95

green Chrysler New Yorker hardtop and drove off south. The starker walked down the corner and stood waiting for the bus.

Dummy walked the short block up the incline to St. Nicolas Avenue and caught the faster Number Three Fifth Avenue bus and was down on 116th Street waiting for the starker. He had resumed his seat on the stool behind the pushcart watermelon stand, and was watching a customer sink his grinning teeth into a quarter of bright red, black-seeded, ice-cold watermelon, when the starker walked rapidly from Seventh Avenue and re-entered the hotel.

Then suddenly Dummy's roving gaze picked up the debonair figure of Slick lounging before the entrance to Sweet Prophet's Temple across the street. Dummy got up, crossed the street and sat on the front stool of a lunch counter, where he could command a view of the whole sidewalk. He pointed to a grill-plate covered with roasting hot dogs. The counter-girl served him one off the front, put it in a bun and slid him the mustard. He then pointed to a shiny nickel-plated juice machine, and the girl drew him a glass of pale yellow liquid called lemon squeeze. He sat there, munching his hot dog in his tongueless mouth and sipping the cold chemical-tasting drink, while watching Slick out of the corners of his eyes.

He noticed that Slick was watching the entrance of the hotel across the street under the pretense of being interested in Sweet Prophet's press clippings, which were on display under glass in the Temple entrance.

Following Slick's gaze, Dummy saw that the starker had reappeared in the hotel entrance, smoking a cigarette. From the way he held the cigarette, pinched between the thumb and forefinger of the right hand, and sucked at it, Dummy knew it was a marijuana cigarette. The starker was watching the entrance to the stairs that led to Sweet Prophet's private quarters, while Slick watched him. There was an intentness about both of them that caused Dummy to wonder.

Suddenly the starker tipped his beaver hat to nothing. Slick stepped quickly from the shadowed entrance of the Temple into the bright sunshine. As he passed the entrance to Sweet Prophet's quarters, a legal size Manila envelope slipped from beneath his coat and fluttered to the sidewalk. He walked a few steps further and paused with his left hand on the handle of a parked car while he fumbled in his pockets with his right hand, as though searching for the keys. No one was close by at the moment, and seemingly no one but Dummy noticed the lost envelope. Nevertheless, the starker kept his gaze riveted on it.

At that moment a buxom colored woman emerged from Sweet Prophet's entrance and stepped from the sidewalk. She stopped for a moment to adjust her tight-fitting cotton print dress more sedately over her corseted figure. She looked like a sister who would say "Amen" at the drop of a hat. The pious expression on her face fought a losing battle with a flaunting pride; her soul was saved, and she knew it. Beneath the bare ham-sized, full black arm she carried a flat, black, narrow attaché case. Her hostile gaze roved over the street scene disapprovingly; then she got astride her dignity and started off.

Her sharp eye lit on the Manila envelope. She started to pass it, but something she saw written on it made her hesitate. She peered with drawn brows, her lips moving slightly as she read. Then suddenly her whole demeanor underwent a complete change. Greed replaced the pious expression on her face. Her dignity gave way to stealth. She looked about furtively to see if she was being watched, then bent over quickly to adjust her shoe. In doing so, the attaché case slipped from beneath her arm and fell directly on top of the envelope, completely hiding it. When she had finished adjusting her shoe and had straightened up with the case, the envelope had disappeared.

Once more the starker tipped his hat to the bright hot sunshine.

Slick turned quickly away from the parked car and approached the woman from the rear.

"I beg your pardon, madame, but I just dropped that envelope," he said politely. "It must have slipped from my pocket while I was putting away my wallet."

The woman looked as offended as though he had said, "Hi, baby, how about a date?" She drew up to her full fat height and said sharply, "What envelope? What are you talking about?"

They were standing in profile, and Dummy could read their lips. He swallowed with a sound like a dog gulping meat.

A slight frown creased Slick's forehead. "The one you just picked up, madame?"

"I didn't pick up any envelope," she said harshly, trying to move off. "And if you don't let me alone, I'll call that policeman."

A uniformed cop was standing down at the corner, twirling his white billy.

But Slick put his hand on her arm, nevertheless, and detained her.

"Now, madame, there is no need of creating a scene," he said smoothly. "I happened to see your reflection in the window of my

97

car when you stooped to pick up the envelope. You are holding it on the other side of that attaché case."

The woman looked suddenly embarrassed. "Oh, *that* envelope!" she exclaimed with a laugh. Then, as she looked him over more carefully, her eyes got small and hard with suspicion. "How do I know it belongs to you?"

"How would I know you had picked it up if I hadn't dropped it?" he countered indulgently.

The woman thought that over, and wasn't satisfied. "All right, if it's yours, then describe it," she demanded.

Slick lost his confident expression. He cleared his throat and said hesitatingly. "It's a brown bank envelope."

The woman pounced on him. "What bank?"

"The Corn Exchange," he said, as though guessing at random.

The woman turned her back and slipped the edge of the envelope from beneath the attaché case far enough to read the return address. Nothing else was written on it.

"Hah!" she exclaimed triumphantly, turning back to confront him. "You didn't see as good as you thought; it's from the Manufacturer's Trust Company."

"That's what I meant," Slick said, putting on a bright smile. "I have money in several banks, and it slipped my mind which bank I had been to this morning."

"It slipped your mind, right enough," she sneered. "Because it don't belong to you, slicker. You just figured I was an ignorant woman and you could beat me out of it, but you figured wrong, mister man."

"Well, it doesn't belong to you either," Slick said, losing philosophically. "And my only purpose in accosting you was to see that it is returned to its owner. No one up here in Harlem can afford to lose that much money."

Her eyes narrowed. "How do you know how much money is in it," she demanded, her cupidity getting the better of her logic.

"Let's count it and see," he suggested reasonably.

"What for?" she asked with growing resentment.

"So we can divide it," he said frankly.

"I'm a law-abiding, religious woman," she said, getting on her high horse. "I'm not going to have anything to do with you."

"Then I'll call the policeman on the corner and tell him what you found," he said indifferently.

"Wait a minute," she said hastily. "Let's see how much there is, first."

98

She turned her back and drew forth the envelope, but he demanded, "Let me see, too."

Reluctantly, she allowed him to watch her while she opened the flap and looked at the contents. A sheaf of bright green bank notes tied with a paper band peeped out of them.

She started to pull it out but he stopped her quickly. "Watch out – don't show it. Somebody will see and get suspicious. Just leaf back the edges."

They both looked about and up and down the street, then moved closer together to form a screen. She slid the edges of the notes out far enough to show the hundred-dollar marker. She gasped. Her lips moved slightly as she leafed the notes back one by one. Her hand trembled. "My God," she whispered. "Twenty thousand dollars."

"Put them back," he cautioned.

She pushed the notes back into the envelope.

"Ten thousand apiece," he breathed. Taking a Manila envelope of similar shape and size from his inner pocket, he said, "You give me the envelope and keep your eye on the policeman while I take out my half."

Sight of the similar envelope combined with the artfulness of his request reawakened her suspicion.

"Naw you don't,' she said in a strident voice, clinging to the envelope and drawing away from him. "You must take me for a square. I know all about you slick con men switching envelopes."

A look of extreme disgust contorted his features. "Here, woman," he said, handing her the envelope. "You divide it. I never saw anyone so suspicious."

But his ready acquiescence inspired her with cunning. Her face took on a look of sanctimonious concern. "We had better wait," she suggested in an earnest voice. "Maybe Sweet Prophet lost it. He's the only person around these parts who ever has that much money, and I don't want to take nothing of him. I had better take it upstairs and ask him."

"I'll go with you," he said quickly.

"No, you had better not," she said. "He'll get suspicious if he sees me bringing in a stranger, and he'll take it away from both of us and turn it over to the police."

"Listen, woman," he said, getting tough. "Do you think I'm going to trust you out of my sight with my ten thousand dollars?"

She thought for a moment, and her eyes got small as ball bearings. She thrust the attaché case toward him and said, "Here, you keep this bagful of money if you don't trust me. It's Sweet Prophet's weekend take, which I was taking to the bank. I'll bet there's more money in there than there is in this envelope anyway."

Reluctantly, he accepted the case. "All right, I'm going to trust you this time," he said. "But don't you try to double-cross me, because, if you do, I'll keep the money in this bag."

"Oh, you can trust me," she lilted triumphantly as she turned away. "I believe in what is right."

He watched her pass through the entrance and start up the stairs. Then he turned and walked quickly toward his own car parked farther down the street, passing in back of Dummy without noticing him. At the same time the starker quit his post in the hotel entrance across the street, hastened down the opposite sidewalk and cut across the street to pile quickly into the back of Slick's car. The car started, and they drove off.

Dummy jumped from his stool and sprinted down the street. He turned in past the exit doorways of the theater where he had met the detectives earlier, and came out into an alley between the two streets. He was in time to see the big dark woman in the print dress come stealthily from the back entrance of Sweet Prophet's house. She turned toward Seventh Avenue, hurrying along. He followed her.

She caught a Number Three Fifth Avenue bus at 110th Street, and he just managed to get in behind her. She got off at 145th Street and Convent Avenue and walked over to Broadway. He was right behind her. She entered a branch of the Chase National Bank and stopped at the window of a receiving teller. When her turn came, the teller smiled and greeted her. "Good morning, Sister Hopeful, how is Sweet Prophet?"

"Fine and dandy," she said happily. "He wants to put three thousand dollars in the bank."

She passed him the deposit slip, already made out, and thirty bright green, brand-new hundred-dollar bills.

He looked at the top note, and his eyes widened in incredulity. Quickly he thumbed them back, staring at each in turn, his eyes becoming wider and wider. Then, very much as the Jew had done, he doubled over and began to laugh. He couldn't help it; he knew the cashier would give him hell, but what could he do?

Finally he said in a strangled voice, "You are ninety-four years late and in a different country."

She continued to grin; she didn't know what he meant.

"This is Confederate money," he explained.

"Confederate money," she echoed stupidly.

"Money issued by the Confederate states – the South – during the Civil War. It is not legal tender any more, I'm afraid."

Numb with shock, she reached over slowly and picked it up and stared at it. "It do look different, don't it?" she said stupidly. "And you say it ain't worth nothing?"

"Well," he said hesitantly, "It's valuable as a souvenir – if you're from the South."

All of a sudden, her eyes popped from their sockets as though they had exploded. Her face turned gray. Her mouth opened wide. Sound came from it – a lot of sound.

"I been robbed!" she screamed. "I been swindled. That black son of a bitch has done beat me out of all my Christian money!"

It required the efforts of two bank guards to subdue her and send her to the police station to tell her story.

Dummy stole quietly away.

16

At ten o'clock, Alberta was arraigned before the Municipal Court and bound over to the Grand Jury. Her bail was set at $2,500. No one was there to go her bail.

She was transferred downstairs from the city prison to the county prison. They are both in the same building, because Manhattan is a county as well as one of the boroughs of New York City.

She was mugged and fingerprinted, and her Bertillon measurements were taken. Then she put in a cell with a light yellow sloppy-looking woman serving a year and a day for shoplifting.

"The top bunk, dearie," the yellow woman said.

Alberta climbed up into the top bunk and lay down.

"What's your rap, dearie?" the yellow woman asked.

"I ain't got any rap," Alberta muttered.

"What are you down for, then?"

"I ain't down for nothing."

"That ain't going to get you nowhere, dearie, acting like that. You've got your mouth stuck out a country mile."

"What if I is," Alberta said.

The yellow woman laughed maliciously. "You'll get used to it, dearie. I've been down so long that down don't worry me."

"I want to see my preacher," Alberta said.

"Who is your preacher, dearie?"

"Sweet Prophet."

"That old hustler."

"Don't talk like that about my preacher," Alberta said.

"He ain't no preacher," the yellow woman said. "He's a pimp."

Alberta got down from her bunk and stood over the yellow woman. Her face was puffed up, and she looked threatening.

"You take that back," she demanded.

The yellow woman sized her up. "All right, dearie. I was wrong," she said. "Have you got any money?"

"I got fifty dollars," Alberta said.

"You have, honey!" the yellow woman exclaimed in a sugary

voice. "You got fifty bucks. Why, honey, you just give me half of it and I'll get word to your preacher."

"How are you going to do that?" Alberta asked suspiciously.

"It's easy. You just got to grease the right palm. What's the old – er – prophet's phone number?"

"I don't know."

"Well, it don't make any difference, if he's in the book. You just give me the money and relax."

"I ain't got nothing but ten-dollar bills," Alberta said.

"Well, just give me thirty dollars," the yellow woman said. "It ain't going to break you."

Alberta fished three ten-dollar bills from her brassiere and handed them to the yellow woman.

"If he don't come, I want my money back," she said.

"I can't do no business like that, honey," the yellow woman said as she stuffed the bills into the toe of her shoe. "Use your head. All I can do is to get word to him; if he don't come, it won't be my fault."

Alberta gave in. "All right. Maybe he won't have time to come, but just tell him to get me out of here."

"I'll sure tell him that, honey," the yellow woman promised.

She raked her tin cup across the bars, then lay on the floor and writhed and screamed.

Shortly, a big Irish matron appeared.

"I got the cramps," the yellow woman gasped. "I feel like I'm dying."

"All right, just relax," the Irish matron said. "If you ain't died yet from the cramps, you won't die now. I'll call Mrs. Ball to take you to surgery."

When the matron left, the yellow woman winked at Alberta and said, "You got to learn that if you're in here for any length of time. The only thing they'll take you to surgery for right away is the cramps. After you get there, you can make any connections you want."

"I just want to see my preacher," Alberta said. "He'll tell me what to do."

17

Sugar Stonewall was in the courtroom when Alberta was bound over. It was safe enough. Half of the spectators were colored people who looked just like him. Still, he was tense.

He had begged his subway fare downtown. Now he stopped a colored woman in the corridor and asked, "Lady, can you give me fifteen cents to get uptown? I just ain't got no money."

She fished a subway token from her purse and handed it to him without looking up.

He stopped on the way out and drank from the fountain. Water wouldn't nourish him, he knew, but it helped to weight his empty stomach down.

He walked over to Broadway and caught the A express train, transferred to a local at 125th Street and rode back to ll6th Street.

It was about eleven o'clock when he arrived at the tenement on 118th Street where Alberta had her flat.

The big black woman hanging out of the front window on the ground floor was beginning to show signs of wear. The sun was on that side of the street, and her eyes blinked sleepily in the sunshine, but she was still hanging on with grim determination.

Sugar tried to slip past her, but she opened her eyes and caught him.

"I thought you'd be in jail by now," she said by way of greeting.

"Why don't you leave me alone, woman," he muttered.

"I ain't doing nothing to you," she said, taking offense. "It ain't none of my business what you people do."

He entered the hall without replying. He kept going, up to the roof, and paused for a moment at the top of the fire escape to case the windows on the other side of the back court. Most of the windows were wide open, and housewives were visible doing their Monday morning chores. The weekly washings were strung on pulley lines from one building to another, crisscrossing one below the other down the narrow pit to the bottom. The graveled tar of the flat, burning hot roof was soft beneath his feet.

Finally he relaxed. He was on familiar ground. The heat

bubbling from the tarred roof, the smell of cooking collard greens and pork and the jarring clash of colors on the lines of Monday wash put him at his ease.

He went down the fire escape and tried the window. A woman watched him from the kitchen window across the courtyard, but she had seen him in the flat often enough to know him. The shades were drawn and the window was locked, but he had long before prepared for such an emergency. A tiny hole was chipped in the window glass just above the catch, and a rusty tenpenny nail was wedged in the corner between the window frame and sill, where he had left it.

He opened the latch, raised the window and went inside, slipping beneath the shade. The woman across the way lost interest and returned to her chores when she didn't hear any sounds of fighting.

He discarded his sweat-stained rayon jacket and dirty straw hat and went to work. He searched every nook and cranny in the three rooms, going about it methodically. He examined every board in the floor, the baseboards, probed all the rat holes. He even pried loose the tin can tops nailed over the larger rat holes and speared in the openings with a fork. He went through the closet and the cupboards, moving the dishes and the utensils, and the cans, boxes, cartons and stacks of old paper sacks to look underneath them. He emptied the containers of salt and flour, sugar and corn meal, dried peas and hominy grits, and refilled them one by one. He searched the fire-box of the potbellied stove in the sitting room, the oven of the gas stove in the kitchen, inside the electric refrigerator and underneath.

Then he dumped the shoe box containing the policy slips and studied them. They didn't give him any clue.

Two hours later he was convinced the money wasn't there. He was beginning to doubt whether there had been any money. The only thing left to do was to go back and try to find Mabel. It wasn't likely that Rufus had given her any large sum of money to keep for him, but she might know something. The trouble was getting in to see her.

From the kitchen window he could see the people in the various kitchens across the courtyard sitting down to eat. He figured this would be a good time to call on Mabel. But he was so tired and hungry his wits were blunted. He figured he ought to eat first. He had seen food in the refrigerator but had not paid it any attention.

Now he explored it again. He found three pork chops, two eggs, a saucepan half-filled with cold hominy grits and a serving dish containing dandelion greens and okra that had been boiled with pigs feet. The pigs feet had already been eaten.

He got out the big iron skillet, poured in some half rancid drippings from the lard can on the back of the stove and put the chops on to fry. While they were frying, he pried the hominy grits from the saucepan in one piece, and cut it into slices an inch thick.

When the chops were done he added more drippings, fried the hominy grits a rich brown, stacked them alongside the chops and fried eggs country style. He put the fried eggs on top of the grits and dumped the greens and okra into the pan, bringing it just to a boil.

He left everything on top of the stove and ate, standing, until it was all gone. By then he was so sleepy he couldn't keep his eyes open.

He went into the bedroom, stretched out on the floor with his head on the pile of Alberta's lingerie and went to sleep.

Twenty minutes later he was snoring loud and steadily. When he exhaled, his snores sounded like a herd of buffalos drinking water; when he inhaled they sounded like a round saw cutting through a fat pine knot. His mouth was open, and a bottle fly was crawling about the crater as though trying to get up nerve to take the plunge. Every now and then Sugar would strike at it limply with his right hand, but he only succeeded in knocking his bottom lip out of shape.

He didn't wake up when the window was slowly raised by someone on the fire escape. He didn't see the man slide cautiously underneath the shade and enter the room.

The man had an open knife in his hand. It had a heavy, brutal-looking blade about seven inches long. The man approached on tiptoe and looked down at his face. He chased the fly with his shoe, but Sugar didn't stir.

The man tiptoed to the door and looked into the kitchen; then he tiptoed to the other door and looked into the sitting room. Then he went back, stood over Sugar and watched him sleeping. He looked as though he were trying to make up his mind about something.

After a while he knelt down beside Sugar and placed the knife on the floor within easy reach. He took his time searching all of Sugar's pockets.

All this didn't even cause a break in Sugar's snoring.

The man did not even smile. Obviously he had no sense of humor.

He picked up the knife and stood up. Still holding the knife open and ready, he scrounged out of the window backwards and went up the fire escape, leaving the window open.

18

A short time after Sugar arrived at the tenement on 118th Street, Dummy arrived back on 116th Street.

The clock in the window of the credit jeweler's said: 11.27.

Dummy kept along that side of the street until he came to the hotel. After looking about in all directions, he entered the hotel like a minister ducking into a house of prostitution. He climbed the smelly stairs to the fourth floor.

It was hot and airless beneath the low, flat, tarred roof, and the heat brought out stinks from the half-rotten floor that had been buried for decades.

A heavy brass padlock hung from the staples screwed to the door frame, but the wood where the hinge of the hasp was screwed to the door looked weakened by previous screw holes. Dummy could have broken through the flimsy door with his shoulder, but it was too risky at that time of the day. He hadn't brought along anything to pry loose the hasp because he had been expecting to find a simple warded lock.

In exasperation he snatched at the big brass lock, and it came open in his hand. His mouth gaped open in a grunting laugh. Ninety-nine people out of a hundred confronted with that lock would have attempted to break open the door, he thought; and hardly anyone would spot that it was a phony. Not a bad idea if you couldn't afford a lock that worked, he thought.

He removed the lock, pushed the door open and walked in. The occupant hadn't taken the trouble to bother with the warded lock.

The room stank with the scent of stale reefer fumes and the rank body odors that collect in stagnant air. A green window shade was drawn over the single tightly closed window, but sunlight filtered through the cracks in it to form an abstract pattern on the dirt-gray sheet that covered the three-quarter bed. A corner was curtained off for a clothes closet by a sleazy curtain, faded with age. In another corner was a wash basin the size of a bird bath; the single tap dripped cold water that left an indelible rust stain on the white enamel. Dirt encrusted the linoleum floor.

Dummy closed the door and snapped up the shade, flooding the room with hard bright sunlight. The light couldn't hurt it.

Dummy looked beneath the bed. He found the remains of a cotton mattress that had been split down the middle and the padding pulled out and stuffed back in. He began grunting with excitement, making a sound like a hog guzzling swill.

He left the mattress where it was and gave his attention to a warped, scarred pasteboard suitcase lying flat on the floor against the inside wall. The lock didn't work, and the snaps weren't fastened. He lifted the lid and poked about in an accumulation of dirty cotton socks and underwear, holding his nose with his other hand. He didn't bother to close the suitcase. He crossed the room, drew open the sleazy curtain and examined the few soiled garments draped over wire hangers hanging from a sawed-off broomstick. The clothes took more of his time than anything else. But, even so, he was finished in under five minutes.

He was relieved to get out of the room, but his muscles didn't relax until he had quit the hotel and put a block's distance in between.

Around the corner on Lenox Avenue, a smooth-looking curly-haired young man sat in a two-toned Buick hardtop parked at the curb. Colored men and women approached him at the rate of one every ten seconds and handed him a canvas bag of money and a rubber-bound scratch pad, the size of a playing card, filled with pages of numbers.

He was a pickup man for a numbers house. Two hard-faced, oversized colored men sat in a black Mercury sedan parked directly behind him. They were the bodyguards hired by the house.

Dummy stopped to write in his scratch pad. He tore out the sheet and approached the pickup man. Before he got there, one of the big colored men in the Mercury opened the door and hit the pavement. No sooner had Dummy passed the written sheet to the pickup man than the bodyguard clutched the back of his neck.

"It's just Dummy," the pickup man said.

"I know it's Dummy," the bodyguard man said. "Since when did he get to be one of our writers?"

"He wants to know where we're drawing today," the pickup man said.

Since the police had tightened up on gambling, the lottery was floated to a different place every day.

"Don't tell him nothing," the bodyguard said. "He's a stool pigeon."

A writer squeezed ahead with his bag of money and play slips and the pickup man said, "Woodbine."

The bodyguard gave Dummy a push, and the pickup man didn't look at him again. Dummy gave no sign that it mattered.

Fifteen minutes later he got out of a taxi in front of a hotel way uptown in the Harlem Heights on St. Nicholas Avenue near 154th Street. The sign over the entrance read *Hotel Woodbine*. Dummy paid the driver and went inside.

Two men came in with heavy luggage and were sent to a suite reserved in advance. Two women followed with modernistic cases that might have been sound recorders and were sent to the same suite. They came in taxis, two at a time, well-dressed men and women, until the entire staff of sixteen had arrived.

Four bodyguards took seats about the lobby, one of them in the chair beside Dummy. He leaned over and whispered through his cupped hand, "Don't dig your grave, stoolie."

Dummy got up and moved to another chair. He knew the setup, and he was not interfering. Upstairs in the two-room suite, the office staff would set up four adding machines and an electric addressograph. There were eight pickup men, who collected the play slips and money from two hundred number writers. The pickup men turned in the books to the women operating the adding machines. The totals were tabulated and checked against the money turned in.

While this was taking place, two men set up the drawing machine. It was a small felt-lined keg with a sliding door, mounted on a winch and turned by a crank. Small black balls made of gutta-percha, lettered in luminous white paint from 0 to 9 – three of each number, making thirty figures altogether – were put into the keg, and the door securely closed. The crank was turned over ten times, the door was opened and a blindfolded man put his hand in the keg and drew out one ball. This was repeated three times, and the three numbers thus drawn, in the order in which they were drawn, comprised the winning number for that day.

The blindfolded man who drew the number was not a member of the staff. A different man was picked each day from among the two hundred writers or from the regular players.

When the number was drawn the play slips were rapidly checked and the winning slips put aside for the payoff.

Then the addressograph was set with the name of the house and the winning number:

As many slips – called hit-slips – were printed as time would allow.

The winning play slips were paid off and assembled in eight collections. The equipment was repacked. The office staff, the man who drew and the eight pickup men left hurriedly. The operator and his two lieutenants remained to wait for the eight payoff men, who took the place of the pickup men. The payoff men arrived, collected the payoffs and left. The operator and his lieutenants came out last with the take.

Dummy watched them come and go. He knew that, in addition to the four bodyguards in the lobby, there were two more in the Mercury sedan outside and probably others stationed out of sight. He didn't make any sudden moves, but he timed his movements so that he was just leaving as Slick came down and started out the door.

He slipped Slick a sheet of paper from his scratch pad on which was written: *the punk is doublecrossin you.*

Slick glanced at it, looked up quickly at Dummy and said, "Come on," with the quick, sure decision of a man who knew the score. The pale yellow eyes sent a chill down Dummy's spine. He obeyed automatically.

They went down the stairs, and Slick nodded in the direction of 154th Street. He walked a little apart from Dummy, on the right side and a little apart. The two guards in the Mercury sedan never took their eyes from them. Nothing was said.

They walked in silence to the corner, and Dummy glanced at Slick for directions. Slick bent his head in the direction of his car, parked two doors up the street.

They arrived at the Chrysler hardtop, and Slick said in a low, controlled voice, "Stand still a moment."

Dummy had his back turned and was facing the car. He didn't see the motion of Slick's lips, and he had taken it for granted that Slick wanted him to get into the car. He put his hand on the door handle and he had started to open the door when suddenly he felt a hand grip his shoulder and his body spun violently around.

Up the street a motor roared, and a car sped down the incline and cut in front of the Chrysler with dragging brakes. A big scar-faced Negro in a red sport shirt and a Panama straw was out of the door and in the street with a snub-barreled .38 revolver in his hand before the car stopped skidding.

Dummy felt his guts shrink.

"I'll handle it," Slick said coldly to the gunman. "It's a private matter."

"You're new here, son, so I'll tell you," the gunman said in a flat Southern voice. "There ain't no private matter when you're carryin' the house money."

Slick ignored him. "You're a dummy, eh?" he said to Dummy.

Dummy nodded.

"You can read lips, though."

Again Dummy nodded.

"Put your fingertips on your shoulders and your elbows out," Slick ordered.

Dummy did as he was ordered.

Slick frisked him with quick, sure movements.

"He's clean," he said to the gunman.

"Watch out for him," the gunman said, getting back into the car. "He might be a stoolie."

Slick gave him a thin, cold smile.

Two colored men were passing on the opposite side of the street. They made as though they hadn't seen a thing.

The front car backed up and pulled up by the corner.

Slick went around and got behind the wheel of his Chrysler and turned south on Saint Nicholas Avenue. Far down the incline of the black-topped avenue, stretching toward the east, rooftops in the Valley of Harlem could be seen.

Slick turned toward Dummy as they purred past the basement entrance to Bucky's Cabaret and asked, "What makes you think so?"

Dummy made motions like writing and pointed toward his pocket. He wasn't taking any chances. Slick smiled thinly and nodded. Dummy fished out his stub of pencil and dirty scratch pad.

He wrote: *he got the mattress in his room all cutup   money was in it*, and held it up for Slick to read.

"How do you know that?" Slick asked.

i seen it Dummy wrote.

"No, I mean the money," Slick said.

it figgers   the money was gone before the jew got there, Dummy wrote.

Slick pulled up for a red light at 145th Street. A real cool black chick in a beige blouse and aqua slacks gave him the eye. But he had business on his mind.

"How do you figure that?" he asked Dummy as he started up again.

Dummy wrote rapidly: *nobody aint found it   he didn get mattress from the jew   must got it afore the jew got there   rufus didn get it   that for sure.*

"It ain't for sure he got it, either," Slick said. "The bitch might have hid it somewhere else. She might still have it – how do you know?"

Dummy began grunting with excitement, *no she aint got it   she lookin for it.*

"How do you know she's looking for it?" Slick asked. "She's in jail. Can you read minds?"

Dummy made sounds like a stopped-up drain. He started to write, but he didn't have space on that sheet and tore it off. Slick reached for it, drew it from his fingers and slipped it into his side . coat pocket.

Dummy wrote on the clean sheet: *i seen her fore she got rested   she come see my cassie   looking for rufus she say   i know better   she looking for money.*

Slick's face didn't show any signs of heightened interest, but his hands tightened on the steering wheel.

"Did she tell your woman she had hid the money in the mattress?" he asked.

she didn tell nothin but we knew   had to be sumthin sides just her furniter the way she look, Dummy wrote.

"That still don't figure absolutely that he got it," Slick said.

somebody got it and he the only one could of, Dummy wrote.

"Why hasn't he cut out if he's got it?" Slick asked. "What's he hanging around for?"

what he got the civil war money for, Dummy countered.

Slick laughed. "You're doing the talking," he said.

he trying to con you to thinkin he aint got it, Dummy wrote.

Slick's face got cold and hard. "That's easier said than done," he concluded, reached over, tore the sheet from Dummy's pad and put it into his pocket with the other sheet. "Now just sit here and be still," he ordered. "I got work to do."

They were approaching 125th Street, and Slick became alert to his surroundings. He was the payoff man for the district between 125th Street and 116th Street, bound on the west by Manhattan Avenue and on the east by Lenox Avenue.

"And if you spot any snoopers, point them out," he added. "If you're a stool pigeon like they say, you ought to know them all."

Dummy made as if he were looking somewhere else and didn't get it.

112

Slick wore a money belt divided into pockets, in which he carried the payoff money, the winning slips and hit-slips. He stopped off at the numbers drops in barber shops, pool rooms, tobacco stores and shoe-shine parlors along the way, and met the roving writers in hallways and parked cars or in their flats. He kept five per cent of the payoff for his end on the small, everyday hits, but on the big hits, which he had to deliver in person to the winner, he kept ten per cent. The writers delivered the small payoffs and kept ten per cent for their end. Only the office staff, the pickup men and the guards were on salaries; the others took their commissions out of the winnings.

It was two-seventeen by the clock in the window of the credit jeweler's on 116th Street when Slick finished his rounds. He pulled up on the opposite side of the street, a half block's entrance from Sweet Prophet's Temple of Wonderful Prayer, and parked. He wasn't concerned about the woman they had beat earlier. She would be looking for a man in a black Buick sedan, the car beside which he had been standing when she first saw him. The way he thought about it, if he had to hide from all the squares he had beat, he could never show himself on the street.

Dummy saw the starker when he turned in from Seventh Avenue. He was wearing the same ensemble – beaver hat, tweed jacket, mustard-colored corduroy pants and cowboy boots.

Slick saw him, too, in the rear-view mirror.

The starker crossed the street, jaywalking through the traffic, and rounded the Chrysler to get into the front seat beside Slick. Then he saw Dummy and seemed to freeze.

"Get in the back seat," Slick said.

He got into the back seat.

"Dummy, this is Susie," Slick said. "Susie, this is Dummy."

Neither moved or made a sound to acknowledge the introduction.

"We're going uptown to my pad and have a little talk about a matter of interest to us all," Slick said, and put the ignition key in the lock, starting the motor.

Susie took a marijuana butt from behind his ear and lit it.

Dummy sat with his hands on his knees and his head moving continuously from one side to the other.

Slick accelerated the car slowly and slid into the stream of traffic.

19

A woman let them in to the third-floor apartment in Roger Morris. Dummy's hope of catching sight of his deaf porter friend in the vestibule hadn't borne fruit. He would have signaled him a message, if no more than to say "Watch out."

He experienced an infinite dread of going unarmed to a strange apartment with Slick and Susie. The woman did nothing to allay it.

Dummy thought that she was a very strange woman. Ordinarily she would have looked like any other sepia-colored well-kept women, of which there were millions. But her hair was dyed bright yellow and pulled so tightly in a severe bun at the nape of her neck that it stretched the skin about her eyes, making the lids slant like an Oriental's. She wore a high-necked, tight-fitting Chinese gown of deep purple silk. She was thin, but she didn't look anemic. Her nostrils had a pale pinched look, and the pupils of her brown eyes were so distended her eyes looked almost black. She carried her head unnaturally high, and she didn't speak. Silently she led them down a close-smelling, almost pitch-dark hall, past several closed doors, to the front sitting room.

It was a big room with three windows overlooking Edgecombe Drive and the rocky clifflike park dropping to the flats bordering Harlem River; in the distance the streets of West Bronx could be seen, rising like a terraced landscape fashioned of bricks.

In the brighter light Dummy saw at a glance that she was a junky; that she sniffed cocaine; that she had been sniffing it for so long she didn't know what life was without it and couldn't live such a life for one full day. That didn't worry him; but her silence did. That and something else about her that he couldn't figure. She never looked directly at anyone.

"Sit down," Slick ordered the two of them, and sprawled onto a chaise longue flanked by a glass-topped cocktail table. To the woman he said, "Fix my pipe and bring my rod."

The woman moved, as though flowing, through another door into another room.

Susie and Dummy found chairs on opposite sides of Slick, as far apart from each other as possible. Dummy sat on the edge of his seat with his feet drawn back and his leg muscles tense, as though prepared to leap in any direction the occasion demanded. But Susie sat sprawled out in his seat – his legs extended, his cowboy boots crossed and the brim of the beaver hat pulled down over his eyes, as though to give the impression he had been there before and was not impressed.

However, it was an impressive room. The furniture didn't match and didn't fit, but every piece was expensive and unusual. Everything, including the curtains and drapes – with the exception of the console radio-record player-television set – had been stolen at one time or another, and Slick had bought it hot.

Dummy's gaze roved from one piece to another. The furniture seemed to be trying to tell him something, but he didn't know what.

No one spoke. The silence oppressed Dummy and put his nerves on a screaming edge. Susie lit a fresh stick of marijuana, took out his knife and began strapping the blade on his boot. Slick didn't seem to be bothered at all.

The woman returned, moving so silently across the carpeted floor that no one saw her until she stood beside the cocktail table flanking Slick's chair. She placed a round, ivory-coloured plastic tray on the glass top. The tray held a small nickel-plated alcohol lamp and a water-cooled pipe. The metal bowl rested on the alcohol lamp, and the bit was stuck into a coil of transparent tubing like the head of a sleeping snake. Nestled among the rest was a flat, vicious looking, blued-steel eleven-shot .38 caliber Colt automatic pistol.

The gazes of both Susie and Dummy focused on the pistol and didn't leave it.

The woman took the opium pill from her pocket, kneaded it skillfully with slim, delicate fingers and shaped it into a tiny ball. She fitted the ball into the shallow cavity of the metal bowl and lighted the alcohol lamp, and at the first bubbling of the pill she picked up the bit, unfurling the tube, and placed it between Slick's lips.

Four puffs and it was finished.

The woman cleaned up and removed the tray, leaving the pistol on the glass top. She flowed silently from the room without having once looked directly at anyone.

Slick lay back with his eyes half closed and seemed lost to the world. The silence ran on. He didn't give the impression of having any intention of breaking it.

Dummy swallowed nervously, making a sound like a baby

burping. Susie gave a violent start and jerked up the knife. Slick looked over at Dummy sleepily.

'Don't make so much noise," he said in a slow lazy voice.

They sat waiting. The silence got on Susie's nerves. The windows were closed against the heat, and the room was in the shade. But the air was motionless, and a haze of marijuana smoke collected about Susie's head.

Dummy could sense the silence, although he couldn't hear it. His eyes rolled in their sockets, and his head turned slowly from side to side as though controlled by an eccentric gear. He looked at the knife in Susie's hand; his gaze traveled upward to Susie's face, then turned and ran along the wall, passed over pieces of furniture and focused for a time on Slick's face; it traveled down the length of Slick's reclining body, then slowly returned over the same orbit.

Slick gave himself twenty minutes for the hop to settle comfortably in his head. Then he came suddenly to life.

"Now," he said briskly, sitting up.

He picked up the automatic pistol, ejected the clip, saw that it was fully loaded, looked at the cartridge in the chamber and reinserted the clip. The safety was on; he snapped it off and laid the pistol back atop the table within easy reach.

"What d'you think of this?" he asked in a conversational tone of voice, took the first of the three pages from Dummy's scratch pad and held it out toward Susie.

Susie stared at it. His babyish face did not change expression. No intelligence showed in his dilated eyes.

The play took Dummy by surprise. He hadn't expected that development. He had overplayed his hand. Now he was caught running a bluff, facing two armed men – and all he had were his fists. The fists of a prize fighter are considered lethal weapons in New York, but they won't stand up to a gun and a knife.

His body froze and his intestines knotted into a hard lump of gristle. Except for his gaze jerking back and forth from the sheet of paper to Susie's face, he might have been petrified. Now was the time when he needed all his wits, but his brain felt frozen, too.

"Here, rockhead, take it and read it," Slick said to Susie. "And get your brains thawed out; you're going to need them."

Susie stood up slowly, stepped over to Slick and took the paper in his left hand. He looked vaguely puzzled. The dead marijuana butt was glued to his bottom lip like a shred of stained paper, and he held the open knife in his right hand like a riding crop. From a sitting position he looked bigger than he actually was; his shoulders looked a mile wide, and his legs resembled building piles.

His lips moved as his slow, drugged mind spelled out the words: *the punk is doublecrossin you.*

He frowned and looked down at Slick. The cold, repelling expression on Slick's face made him blink. It was obvious that he didn't get it. He read the line again.

"Do it mean me?" he asked incredulously.

Slick didn't answer.

Susie's gaze swung to Dummy. He pointed with the forefinger of the hand in which he held the note as though aiming a pistol. "He wrote it," he said thickly.

All of a sudden he went berserk. His babyish face contorted with insensate rage. He leaped at Dummy and cut at his face with a slashing motion. It went so fast no one was prepared. The big brutal blade moved faster than sight.

A hair-raising noise issued from Dummy's tongueless mouth, sounding like a wild horse screaming in terror. But his body moved automatically from an instinct born in the ring. He gripped the arms of the chair and pushed back with both feet, shifting his full weight to his shoulder blades braced against the back of the chair, and kicked out with his feet tight together. The canvas sneakers didn't carry the impact that hard-soled shoes would have, but the pushing power did the trick. They caught Susie at the top of the thighs and sent him crashing backward into the television set as the arc of the slashing blade passed within a fraction of an inch of Dummy's eyes.

With the same motion, Dummy came down on his feet as Susie bounced from the heavy television set as though his flesh were made of rubber. Susie came in, stabbing sideways in strictly an amateur's thrust, and Dummy wove beneath it and right-handed him in the solar plexus. Spit-drenched air spewed from Susie's stretched mouth in a rush of whining sound, and his eyes bugged out.

"Cut it out," Slick said in a level voice as he picked up the automatic pistol.

Dummy didn't see him, and Susie didn't hear him. Susie moved in a rage that didn't need breath and stabbed backhanded at Dummy's crouching figure. It was a desperate, unbalanced, half-aimed thrust, but it would have caught Dummy in the back of the neck if he hadn't made a blind, headlong dive. He dove into the cocktail table and smashed to the floor, landing, belly flat, on top of the broken glass.

117

"Cut it out, I said," Slick repeated without moving from his seat. He acted as though he had seen a lot of fights and had command of the situation.

But still Susie didn't hear him. The blood was beating in his ears, and his vision was blurred. He doubled to the floor, retching, his neck muscles swollen and corded from his effort to get his breath.

For a moment the tableau held.

At that moment the woman opened the door and took one step into the room. Her gaze darted about as though to locate the source of the commotion, but she didn't look at anyone in particular.

A sudden pool of silence dropped into the room like an air pocket in a raging storm, and she said in an anxious voice, "Honey, you all right?"

Lying on his belly, Dummy read her lips and felt his hair rise.

Susie got his breath with a sound like hissing steam and straightened up. He saw Dummy and started toward him. Dummy pushed to his feet and ran, doubled over, past the woman and through the door. She didn't look at him, but when he ran past her she screamed.

"I'll kill you," Slick said in a flat, absolute voice.

Susie pulled up as though he had run full tilt into an invisible wall.

"Put that knife away and sit down," Slick ordered. Then he said to the woman. "It's all right, baby."

Susie folded the knife, stuck it into the watch pocket of his corduroy pants, went back to his chair and sat down. But he wasn't looking at Slick; he was looking at the woman and frowning.

"The other one," the woman said hesitantly.

"He's all right," Slick said, adding as though by way of explanation, "he's a dummy."

"Oh," the woman said.

Dummy could be heard working with the locks on the outside door.

The woman returned through the door she had entered and closed it behind her. She lay on the bed, reached over to the bed table and turned up the small gilt radio she had been listening to. Dummy had passed through the room to the hall, but he couldn't get the outside door open.

Finally Slick got up from his seat and went through the other door and down the hall, carrying the pistol loosely at his side. He touched Dummy on the shoulder and said, "You can't get out without a key."

118

It was too dark in the hall for Dummy to read his lips, but Dummy knew what he wanted. He turned, walked docilely ahead of Slick back to the front room and resumed his seat.

Slick returned to the chaise longue, ignoring the broken table. "Let's don't have any more of that," he said. "It disturbs baby." He placed the automatic on the floor beside him, then took the other two pages from Dummy's pad and held them out toward Susie.

"Now read these and let's talk about it," he said.

Susie got up, took the pages, sat down and read them, his lips moving as he spelled out the words.

"Well, what about it?" Slick demanded.

"About what?" Susie muttered sullenly.

"Where's the money?"

"I ain't talking in front of this dummy," Susie said. "He's a stool pigeon."

"So what?"

Susie began to puff up; his neck began swelling as though he were choking, and his cheeks puffed out. "Look man, what is you trying to do?" he challenged. "You and him ain't trying nothing like a frame on me, is you?"

"Not me," said Slick indifferently. "I just want the money."

"Because if you is," Susie went on, "you're going to have to use that rod 'stead of just waving it 'round."

Slick nodded toward Dummy. "Ask him what he's trying to do."

Both of them turned and stared at Dummy. He sat forward on the edge of his seat, gripping his knees with his hand, and looked from one to the other.

"What you want?" Susie asked in a threatening tone of voice.

Dummy shrugged and made a V with the thumb and forefinger of his right hand.

"What's that mean?" Susie asked.

Slick turned his stare back to Susie. "You're not very bright, rockhead," he said. "He wants to cut himself a slice of our pie."

"He's going to get more slices than he's looking for," Susie threatened.

"You worry too much," Slick said. "I know what I'm doing."

"Maybe you does, but I don't," Susie said.

"Let him alone," Slick said. "We might need him."

"Need a stool pigeon?" Susie echoed.

"Why not? If he's really a stool pigeon, it's a damn good thing we got hold of him in time, with what he already knows," Slick pointed out.

"I just ask you, don't oversport yourself," Susie said. "I ain't nobody to play with."

"We got that settled," Slick said coldly. "Now where's the money?"

"Listen, I told you what was what," Susie flared.

Again Slick nodded in the direction of Dummy. "He doesn't believe you."

Susie turned and looked at Dummy again. "You're going to be sorry you ever messed in my business," he promised.

"I'm getting tired of this," Slick said in his flat, deadly voice. "I asked you where was the money."

"I ain't got it," Susie said, giving him a straight answer.

"Okay – I hope you're leveling," Slick said.

"I'm leveling," Susie said.

"Okay, you haven't got it. Let's start from there. What did you find in her joint?"

"Nothing. Her joker had already searched it again before I got there, and if anything was hid there he'd been sure to find it," Susie said.

"How do you know he didn't," Slick asked.

"He didn't," Susie said. "I found him asleep on the floor, and I looked around and saw he'd searched the joint; the I searched him. He didn't even wake up. You can bet if he'd had anything worth stealing, he'd been wide awake."

"Let's get back to the mattress," Slick said.

"I has told you, there wasn't nothing in that mattress," Susie flared angrily.

"So you did," Slick said. "You also said you saw her put it there."

Susie corrected him. "I said I seen her sewing the mattress up. And I took it for granted that would be the only reason she'd be sewing up a mattress in the middle of the night."

"Too bad you didn't get it then," Slick said.

Neither of them noticed Dummy leaning forward with his eyes stretched.

"I couldn't have with her joker hanging 'round," Susie said.

"And it wasn't in the mattress when you got it," Slick said.

"It weren't there, and the side of the mattress had been cut open again," Susie said. "One of them beat me to it," he added. "But I don't know which one."

Grunting sounds issuing from Dummy's mouth drew their attention. He had gotten out his scratch pad and was writing in it.

He got up and showed Slick what he had written.

Slick looked up at Susie. "He says neither of them got it."

Susie's face swelled with sudden rage. "If he keeps on trying to frame me, I'm going to stick him," he threatened again.

Dummy moved away from the broken table so it wouldn't be in his way if he had to protect himself.

Slick reached out a foot and touched him on the leg. "How do you know neither of them got it?" he asked.

Dummy wrote in his pad: *i know alright.*

"He just says he knows," Slick told Susie.

"He knows more than what's good for him," Susie said.

maybe she still got it on her, Dummy wrote in his pad and showed it to Slick.

"Not in jail, she hasn't," Slick said. "And it was you who said she didn't know where it was."

Dummy shrugged.

"Maybe she took it out the mattress and hid it somewhere else," Susie said.

Dummy shook his head in the negative.

"I got a feeling that we ain't being very smart," Slick said.

"You're supposed to be the brains," Susie reminded him.

"That's right," Slick acknowledged. "And I'm going to start using them."

20

Between eight and nine o'clock on weekday evenings Sweet Prophet received in private such of his followers who had problems or wished to make confession and new recruits who wished to arrange for baptisms at some future date.

He sat behind the hand-carved mahogany desk in his sumptuous receiving room on the third-floor of his Temple of Wonderful Prayer, while his supplicants sat in the high-backed period chairs across from him.

Attired in a Geneva gown of canary-yellow silk and a sequined headpiece similar to that seen on the statues of Krishna, he looked like the rising sun. The diamonds in the rings on all his fingers sparkled whenever he gestured, and his long twisted fingernails of rainbow hue squirmed as though alive.

Elder Jones stood at his right side, wearing a fresh white uniform.

His private secretary – a quiet, middle-aged woman of culture – sedately dressed in a freshly laundered black linen frock, stood at his left.

The assistant secretary, who had been entrusted with the weekend income to take to the bank, was still downtown in the Fingerprint Bureau of the Central Police Department examining photos of colored confidence men, trying to pick out the one who had swindled her that morning. She had looked at the mugs of criminals until her head swam, but still she stayed on, afraid to report to the Prophet that his money was lost.

Outside, seen through the open front windows, the day was dying. The street lights were on, and the lights in the show windows of stores and in the hot-box apartments; and the sign lights and automobile lights lit up the many-colored faces of the people crowded on the burning hot sidewalks.

Sweet Prophet's hour of consolation was almost over. He was glad of it; other folks' problems had never seemed so distasteful. Strain showed in his face; his bulging eyes looked worried and harassed. It had been a long day for him; he hadn't been able to sleep again after the detectives' pre-dawn visit.

"Who else is there?" he asked.

"Sister Alberta Wright," Elder Jones replied.

Sweet Prophet looked startled. He hesitated. Finally he sighed and said. "Send the sister in."

Alberta paused just inside the door and stared at Sweet Prophet. She looked downcast and bedraggled in the now-filthy garments in which she had been baptized; but her eyes were wide and alight with hope. Sitting there in his brilliant garb, Sweet Prophet appeared to her as a great shining light that had come into this dark moment of her life.

She fished the last ten dollars from her brassiere, went forward and laid it on the desk in front of him. Wearily, he found a crumb of bread for her in the pocket of his gown and pocketed the money. She put the crumb in her mouth and knelt on the floor.

"Arise, my child," he said.

She got up from her knees and sat forward on the edge of the chair.

"What is troubling you, my child?" he asked.

"I hate to keep bothering you after you have been so good to get me out of jail," she said. "But I'm in big trouble."

"Tell me about it, my child," he said.

"It began with my dream," she confessed. "When I dreamt about those three pies exploding with hundred dollar bills, I knew The Lord had sent me a message. So I went and played twenty dollars on the *money row* in the three biggest houses in Harlem. That was all the money I had, sixty dollars, but I knowed The Lord had sent me a message, and I had faith. And just like I believed, my number popped out like it were sent for, and I hit for thirty-six thousand dollars."

"Thirty-six thousand dollars," Sweet Prophet echoed. "That is a lot of money, child."

"Yes, Sweet Prophet, it sure was," she admitted.

"So the houses have gone back to paying six hundred to one," he remarked.

"Yes, Sweet Prophet, they pays off good if you got the message," she said.

"And you had twenty-nine thousand, four hundred dollars left after paying off the commissions?"

"Yes, Sweet Prophet. I had to give the writers the ten per cent which they collects on a hit, and then I had to give the payoff men from each of the houses a thousand dollars for bringing me my money safely. But how did you know?"

"My child, a prophet must know all the workins of sin in order to combat it," he said.

"But I didn't figure it was no sin if The Lord himself sent me the message," she argued.

"No, my child, the sin was that you took this money which The Lord sent to you for the expiation of your sins and hid it for your own self, instead of bringing it to Sweet Prophet, who would have taken a share for The Lord, and returned you the rest in safety."

"How did you know I hid it?" Alberta asked in surprise.

"My child, a prophet knows everything," he said.

"Then where is it now?" she asked.

"We ain't come to that part yet," he said testily. "You ain't finished your confession."

"I didn't intend to keep it hid, Sweet Prophet," she resumed. "I honestly intended to bring it to you for you to take out The Lord's share; but I hadn't got religion then, and I figured I ought to get religion first and get myself baptized so I could come to you in my purity and place the money at your feet for you to give me back in your bounty what you figured I should have. And besides that, Sweet Prophet, my man was away from home when they paid me off, and I figured it would be no greater sin to put temptation in his way. So I hid the money in my mattress, figuring you wouldn't want to deal with the money of a sinner anyway. And so that's why I came to you early Sunday morning and give you the five hundred dollars –"

"You gave to The Lord through me," Sweet Prophet corrected, to keep the record straight in case of an inquiry by the income tax collectors.

"Yes, Sweet Prophet, gave to The Lord through you," Alberta parroted, "the five hundred dollars for to pay to get baptized."

"And afterwards you dilly-dallied around for so long before performing this duty to The Lord that the money was stolen," he said.

"I weren't dilly-dallying around," she protested. "It was stolen whilst I was in my trance."

"The Lord will forgive you," he consoled her. "The Lord wouldn't be expecting you to guard your money while you were in a trance."

"Yes, Sweet Prophet, I believe The Lord will forgive me," she said. "But The Lord ain't done it yet. All The Lord has done so far is chastise me. And that's what I can't understand. Why would The Lord want to chastise me by letting my money be stolen whilst I was setting in heaven at His feet?"

"You haven't told me all that happened as yet, Sister Wright," Sweet Prophet said. "I can't explain The Lord's actions until I know what you have been up to."

Alberta recounted in detail everything that had happened to her since her release from the morgue.

"Now they are saying I beat out the Jew-man's brains with a hammer and cut my husband's throat with a knife," she concluded.

"If they have charged you with that, you are really in big trouble, Sister Wright," Sweet Prophet admitted. "But you didn't do it?"

"No, Sweet Prophet, I didn't do it," she wailed. "You've got to believe me, Sweet Prophet. I ain't never in all my life hit nobody in the head with a hammer hard enough to kill him, and I didn't cut my husband's throat neither, as much as he deserved it."

"Then why do they think you did it, Sister Wright?" he asked.

"It was because of the knife," she said. "They caught me trying to get rid of the knife I found. They said it was the knife that Rufus had been killed with, and, when I saw it lying there, I thought so, too. I didn't know what had happened. All kinds of thoughts ran through my head. I hadn't seen Sugar, and it came to me all of a sudden he might have found out that Rufus had stole my furniture, and I could see them getting into a fight. I figured maybe Sugar might have stabbed Rufus in self-defense, because it would be just like Sugar to throw away the knife and run."

"If that is what happened, all you have to do is tell the police, and they will arrest Sugar and drop the charges against you," Sweet Prophet said.

"But he didn't do it," she declared. "I'd bet my life he didn't do it. He's so tenderhearted he won't even cut off a chicken's head, and I know he wouldn't have stabbed Rufus all those times."

"Well, there is one good thing that has come out of it," Sweet Prophet consoled her. "The Lord has saved you the trouble and expense of getting a divorce; He has made it possible for you to go and sin no more."

"Well, that much He sure has done," Alberta admitted glumly.

"Do the police know about the money you had hidden?" Sweet Prophet asked her, his thoughts taking another tack.

"I didn't tell them," she said. "I wanted to ask you first whether I ought to."

"No, Sister Wright. If you are innocent, don't tell them about the money," he advised. "If they learn about the money, they will believe for sure that you are guilty."

"But what am I going to do, Sweet Prophet?"

"Are you dead sure you left the money in your mattress?" he asked.

"As sure as I'm sure that I'm setting here and you is setting there," she said.

"Did anyone see you when you hid it?"

"Not unless they got eyes that can see through walls," she contended. "The door was locked and the shades were drawn, and I had put Sugar out of the house for the night."

"How did you know he didn't go back and steal it while you were in your religious trance?" he asked.

"He wouldn't have stole all of it," she declared. "I know my Sugar. He would have been too scared of me to steal all of it. That's why I love him. If I got to work to support him, the least he can do is be scared of me. Besides which, why did Rufus and the Jew-man steal my furniture if they weren't looking for the money? I got sense enough to know my furniture weren't worth nothing to nobody but me."

"How would your estranged husband and the Judaist know about the money if you haven't told anybody, Sister Wright?"

"I don't know, Sweet Prophet. You is the only one I have told, and that's the truth," she said.

"Somebody knew you had it," he persisted.

"I don't know who it could have been," she maintained.

"The man who delivered it knew it," he pointed out.

"But there were three different payoff men, one from each of the houses," she argued.

"One of them must have known that you hit in the two other houses," he stated.

"He didn't find it out from me," she said. "I didn't tell nobody."

"They delivered the money to your home?" he asked.

"Yes, Sweet Prophet, they sent it as soon as the drawings were over."

"But not at the same time?"

"No, Sweet Prophet. The Dollar house sent theirs first. They were drawing in Harlem on Saturday and didn't have far to come. A man called Buddy brought it. Then the Monte Carlo house sent theirs next. They were drawing in the Bronx and had farther to come. A man called Bunch Boy brought theirs. And the Tia Juana house sent theirs last because they were drawing away over in Brooklyn. They got a new man called Slick Jenkins who brought theirs."

"And this Slick Jenkins was the last one to come?" Sweet Prophet asked.

"Yes, Sweet Prophet, but he didn't know I had hit in the other two houses," Alberta said.

"It stands to reason that he found it out in some way, came back and stole your money, child," Sweet Prophet declared.

"I don't see how he could have found out," Alberta contradicted. "He didn't see the other money because I hid it as soon as I got it, and I didn't tell him nothing."

"You must have given yourself away in some manner," Sweet Prophet persisted. "If this Slick Jenkins is accustomed to paying off big hits, then he is accustomed to the winners hiding their money, and he would know just where to look. You probably left your mattress uncovered when you hid the other money."

"That's just it, Sweet Prophet, I didn't hide the money in my mattress at first. I cleaned out a lard can and put the money in that and hid it in the refrigerator. I didn't put it in the mattress until after Sugar had come home and I had put him out. I got to thinking it would be safer if I slept on it; but there weren't nobody around when I hid it, and it was still there when I got up yesterday morning because I took out the five hundred dollars to pay for my baptism, and it was there then."

"Of course, child," Sweet Prophet said. "Slick didn't have a chance to steal it until after you had left for the baptism."

"But what about Rufus and the Jew-man stealing my furniture?" she argued stubbornly. "What did they do that for if Slick had already stole my money."

"Just think about one thing at the time," Sweet Prophet said angrily.

"I'm thinking about it," she muttered. "And it don't seem right. He'd be scared to steal the money. The houses wouldn't have no payoff man who stole back the hits; they'd kill him."

"You said he was a new man."

"He's just new in Harlem. He was doing the same thing for a house in Chicago before he came here, and he'd know better," she contended.

Sweet Prophet lost patience. "Can't you get it through your thick head that he stole your money, woman?" he said angrily. "There is no other way it could have happened."

"If you say he stole it, he stole it," Alberta said, quailing.

"You go to him and tell him to give you your money back," Sweet Prophet commanded her. "You tell him that I said so. Tell him that I said I will call down the wrath of heaven on his head if he doesn't give you back your money. Do you know where he lives?"

"Yes, Sweet Prophet, he lives at Five Fifty-five."

"Then you go up there and get your money back," he concluded.

"Yes, Sweet Prophet," she said docilely.

21

"We should have thought of that before," Grave Digger said.

"It was the Jew who threw us," Coffin Ed reflected. "Taking that furniture apart."

"He's still throwing us," Grave Digger admitted. "But first things first."

"Let's go find her then and lock her up again," Coffin Ed suggested.

"And fast, before somebody gets hurt," Grave Digger said.

Fifteen minutes after Alberta had left Sweet Prophet, the detectives' small battered black sedan pulled up before the entrance.

Sweet Prophet was still sitting behind his desk. He still looked like the rising sun. But the lines of weariness on his pop-eyed countenance had been replaced with a look of fury. He was drinking ice-cold lemonade from a frosted silver pitcher in a cut champagne glass, but the way he gulped it, it didn't seem cold enough to satisfy him.

He greeted the detectives irritably. "It took you long enough to get here."

"How did you know we were coming?" Coffin Ed demanded.

Sweet Prophet wiped his face with his yellow silk handkerchief. "I telephoned for you," he said.

"We didn't get your call, but here we are," Grave Digger said. "What's the beef?"

"My secretary was swindled out of three thousand dollars this morning by a confidence man, right outside of my door, and he hasn't been caught."

The detectives stood in front of his desk with their hats pushed back on their heads. They stared down at him.

Another woman – the gullible secretary – had been added to the scene since Alberta's departure.

"And I was just trying to help him," she said.

Grave Digger addressed Sweet Prophet, ignoring her. "You reported it, didn't you? This morning, I mean."

"I did," the secretary said.

"She reported it," Sweet Prophet hastened to sustain. "She went to the police right after it happened, but I have just now found out about it."

"Then you have done all you can do," Grave Digger said unsympathetically. "We're after another matter. Why did you go Alberta Wright's bail?"

"That woman! She's the plague of my life!" Sweet Prophet exclaimed in exasperation. "I did not go her bail. I would not have gone her bail. I do not know how she got out out of jail. She thinks I went her bail, and I couldn't very well disillusion her. But whoever did go her bail did not do me any favor."

The detectives tensed. Coffin Ed's acid-burned face became grimmer, and a vein began throbbing in Grave Digger's temple. Before it had been necessary to find her; now it was urgent.

"That makes it a horse of another color," Grave Digger said. "You know she's been robbed?"

"Yes, I know all about it," Sweet Prophet admitted. "She came here straight from jail and told me everything."

"She told you that she hit the numbers for thirty-six thousand dollars."

"Yes, and you can take it from me that she is as innocent of those killings as I am," Sweet Prophet said.

"Anybody would be innocent to you with that much money," Coffin Ed remarked.

"That's for later," Grave Digger said roughly. "Where is she now?"

"My God, how do I know?" Sweet Prophet snapped. "I would imagine she's trying to get her money back, if she's got any sense. After what she told me about the payoff, it was as plain as the nose on your face that one of the payoff men named Slick Jenkins stole her money. I sent her to his house to get it back."

"You sent her," Coffin Ed echoed.

The detectives stared at Sweet Prophet incredulously.

"You mean to say you sent her out alone to demand her money from a hoodlum you don't even know, knowing that two men have already been killed about it?" Grave Digger asked, the jugular vein swelling in his neck like corded rope.

"No one is going to hurt that woman," Sweet Prophet said callously. "God takes care of children and fools."

"People will recrucify Jesus Christ for thirty-six grand," Coffin Ed said harshly.

130

"You're getting alarmed over nothing," Sweet Prophet said.

"Leave off!" Grave Digger grated. "Did she say where Jenkins lives?"

"In the Roger Morris," Elder Jones volunteered.

"Let's go," Grave Digger said, striding toward the door, but just before leaving he turned and called to Sweet Prophet. "I don't think much of your Christianity, buddy."

It was forty-four city blocks to the house on Edgecombe Drive, and the streets were filled with traffic. They went up Seventh Avenue with the siren open, scattering cars like ninepins, and turned over to the Drive on the 155th Street Bridge.

The elevator was occupied. They took the stairs two at a time.

The woman in the Chinese gown answered their ring. They stood flanking the door. Coffin Ed had eased his pistol loose in its holster and stood with his hand resting on the butt.

"Yes?" the woman said, opening the door onto a heavy burglar-proof chain. She looked through the crack, but not directly at either of them.

Grave Digger flashed his shield. She didn't look at it.

"Yes?" she asked again, impatiently.

"We want to talk to Jenkins," Grave Digger said.

"Who are you?" she asked.

Both of them looked at her sharply.

"Are you trying to be cute?" Coffin Ed challenged.

"Leave off," Grave Digger said, and told the woman. "We're detectives. Do you want to see our identifications?"

"That's not necessary," she said. "Slick isn't in."

"May we come in and look around?" Grave Digger asked.

"No," she said. "I said he wasn't in."

"You're making life hard for yourself," Coffin Ed said.

"Slick left at a quarter to eight," she said. "He hasn't been back." She closed the door. They heard keys turning and bolts locking.

Coffin Ed looked at the locks as though he might enjoy shooting them off.

"I don't quite dig her," Grave Digger said.

They went down to the lobby and found the doorman, a tall, slender man with a winged mustache and a thin rusty-brown face beneath a yachting cap. His gold-braided purple uniform had been pressed so often it shone like waxed paper.

"We're the men," Grave Digger said, flashing his shield

"You don't have to tell me, boss," the doorman said.

"When did Slick Jenkins leave?"

"Before eight, boss."

Grave Digger and Coffin Ed exchanged glances.

"Alone?" Grave Digger asked.

"No, boss, he had a mugger with him what's been hanging on to him for the past few days."

"Mugger!" Grave Digger echoed. "Give us a rundown."

The doorman gave a pinpoint description of Susie, then for good measure threw in a description of Slick, of Slick's car, and the license number. He conducted a little business on the side peddling marijuana cigarettes, and he figured every little bit he did for the police would help him if he got into a jam.

Grave Digger described Alberta and asked if she'd been there.

"I ain't seen nobody like her, boss, and if I'd seen her I sure wouldn't have forgot her."

"Okay, boy, when Jenkins turns up I want you to telephone the 126th Street Precinct Station and leave word," Grave Digger ordered.

"Right, boss. My name is Sam. Don't forget old Sam, boss."

"What's your racket?" Coffin Ed asked.

"I ain't got no racket, boss; I'm just a peace-loving boy."

"Damn right," Coffin Ed said. "Peace at what price?"

They went back to their car.

"We're either too late or too early," Grave Digger said.

He got the precinct station on the radio telephone and asked Lieutenant Anderson to put out a pickup for Slick Jenkins, giving a description of his car and the license number.

Lieutenant Anderson said that Sweet Prophet had telephoned in to say that Alberta Wright's man, Sugar Stonewall, was there at the Temple.

"Off again, on again," Grave Digger muttered.

They did the forty-four blocks back to 116th Street with the siren blaring.

Sweet Prophet was sitting as though he hadn't moved.

He greeted them with, "He left. I couldn't hold him."

"We've got to get a new car," Grave Digger said, then asked, "What did he want, did he say?"

"He wanted me to go his woman's bail because I had baptized her, but I told him that someone had beat me to it."

"Yeah, somebody wants her out bad," Grave Digger said. Slowly his voice was getting thick. "Did he say where he was going?"

"I sent him up to see Slick Jenkins," Sweet Prophet said. "I told him that I had sent his woman up there, and that was where he was most likely to find her. After that I couldn't hold him."

"You're sitting there trying to play God with these little people," Grave Digger said in a voice that sounded as though his mouth were stuffed with cotton. "And all you're doing is shilling for Clay, the undertaker."

"I'm a busy man," Sweet Prophet said defensively.

"Yeah, but not so busy as you would be breaking up rocks," Grave Digger said, then asked, "What does Stonewall look like, if you weren't too busy to have looked."

Sweet Prophet kept an offended silence, but the two women and Elder Jones gave a composite description.

"Gone again, John again," Grave Digger muttered as he climbed behind the wheel.

They went back up the way they had come; but traffic had thinned considerably on Seventh Avenue, and everyone with a guilty conscience had got in off the street.

In answer to their questions, Sam the doorman said, "Ain't nobody looked like him been through this door, boss, or I would have seen him, and I ain't blind."

"All right, stand out on the sidewalk where we can watch you," Coffin Ed ordered.

"I ain't going to try to tip nobody off," Sam said aggrievedly.

"I don't want to have to worry about it," Coffin Ed said. "I got other things to worry about."

The doorman came out, stood in the center of the sidewalk and didn't move to open the door when the tenants came in and out.

Grave Digger got into their car and eased it to the curb between the racketeers' big shiny cars. It looked out of place. He sat behind the wheel, watching the people pass. He looked out of place. Coffin Ed took up his station on the other side of the entrance, leaning with one hand propped against the top of another big shiny car. He didn't look as though he went with the car, but the people who passed acted as though they didn't notice.

Grave Digger talked to Lieutenant Anderson again, but nothing new had come in.

There was nothing to do but wait. Half of a detective's working time was spent in waiting and watching. They waited and watched.

Twenty minutes later they saw Sugar Stonewall alight from a Fifth Avenue bus and cross the street. Coffin Ed intercepted him and took him by the arm.

"I'm the man," he said.

133

"First time I was ever glad to see the man," Sugar confessed.

Coffin Ed took him to the car and frisked him. Sugar was as docile as a lamb. They put him on the back seat and Coffin Ed sat with him while they drove down to the precinct.

Sugar spoke only once, to ask, "You got a cigarette, chief?"

"Afterwards," Coffin Ed grunted.

They took him in to the Pigeon's Nest and installed him on the wooden stool, beneath the glaring light.

"Talk fast and straight," Grave Digger ordered.

"Yassuh, boss, where do you want me to begin?" Sugar asked.

"You look like a bright boy," Grave Digger said. "Just lead up to it slowly, so we can get the picture. Everything is needed now."

Sugar didn't need any further prompting. Sweat flowed from the creases of his face, and the smell of animal fear emanated from his skin. He talked fast and eagerly.

"It began like this, boss – me and Alberta has been shacking up together for about eight months. Most times when she came home from work at about eight o'clock, I'd be there waiting for her. Weekdays she'd start drinking as soon as she got in – she liked to drink, but she weren't no lush. She'd just sip enough to knock herself out by ten o'clock and I'd help her get to bed. But shucks, I'd just be getting wide awake myself, so I'd go down to the corner and play tonk, and, if I didn't get home 'til three or four the next morning, it wouldn't make any difference to her because she'd be so dead asleep couldn't nothing wake her –"

"You slept all day," Coffin Ed cut in with an outburst of contempt.

"You see, boss, I been sick," Sugar explained.

"For eight months?"

"Let him get to the point," Grave Digger said.

"Well, last Saturday night I got held up in a poker game and didn't get home until after ten o'clock. I figured she was going to be mad all right, because that's when we generally got together, but I didn't expect her to grab me by the collar and throw me out of the house. That's what first made me suspicious, but all I suspected at first was she'd got herself another man. That worried me –"

"I'll bet it did," Coffin Ed cut in again.

"Yassuh, it sure did," Sugar admitted. "So I went down to the bar and thought about it, and the more I thought about it the madder I got. So after a while I crept up on the roof and started to come down the fire escape to sort of spy through the bedroom window. I had made me a little peephole in the window shade in

134

case I was ever going to need it, and I figgered I needed it then. But, when I started to come down from the roof, I saw some joker on the fire escape spying through her window, too. I started to holler at him, but I didn't want –"

"Wait a minute," Grave Digger said. "You saw a man looking through her bedroom window?"

"Trying to, anyway. But he saw me 'bout the same time I saw him, and he took off down –"

"Hold on. You saw this man?"

"Yassuh, but I didn't see him good. The fire escape is in the back, and he was gone on down to the bottom 'fore I could get close to him. I would have chased him, but –"

"Hold on, hold on!" Grave Digger grated. "What did he look like?"

"Like I said, boss, I didn't see him plain but –"

"Big man or little?"

"Big. Rough-looking. Looked like he was young, the way he went down them rungs."

"How was he dressed?"

"I didn't notice too plain, boss. He was wearing a big hat and a coat like everybody else. He was a colored man, that's for sure."

Grave Digger and Coffin Ed looked at one another in silence.

"You think he's lying?" Coffin Ed suggested.

"Let him go on. If he's lying, we'll find out," Grave Digger said.

"And, if you are, it's going to be rough," Coffin Ed promised.

"I ain't lying, boss, I swear before God," Sugar said, knuckling the sweat out of his eyes. "And I couldn't be mistaken, 'cause I seen him again."

"You saw him again?" Grave Digger echoed.

"Yassuh, when I come down the second time I found him in the same place, and he run down to the bottom again like he done before."

"And you didn't see him any better?"

"I forgot to tell you. I seen he had on boots – cowboy boots."

"Boots!" Grave Digger said.

"Yes suh, black and white cowboy boots. I wondered if he belonged to a gang, but I hadn't heard of no gang what wears cowboy boots."

Grave Digger and Coffin Ed exchanged looks again.

'Sounds a little like him," Coffin Ed said.

"Could be," Grave Digger admitted. "It begins to figure." He turned back to Sugar. "How did you figure it?"

135

Sugar looked puzzled. "Him, you mean? I didn't think nothing of it. Just another prowler – that neighborhood is full of prowlers. She didn't have nothing for him to steal – " He broke off. His eyes bucked suddenly, and his jaw dropped open. "Christ almighty, I bet he was after her money!" he exclaimed.

"You just now thought of that?" Grave Digger asked incredulously.

"Well, boss, I admit I've been thinking like a square," Sugar said. "But I hadn't figgered out when I first seen him that she had any money. I was looking for another joker in her bed. So I just figgered he was another prowler, and I didn't give him no more thought."

"All right, all right – if you're lying, we're going to find it out," Grave Digger said. "So when did you figger out she had some money?"

"Well, when I seen she didn't have no other joker in her bed, I figgered she must have got hold of some money, because that's the only reason she'd have for throwing me out the house – to keep me from finding out. Then when I seen her praying –"

"Praying!" Coffin Ed exclaimed.

"Yassuh, boss, she was kneeling beside the bed with her arms hanging down, praying. I figgered right away then she had hit the numbers for a big stake. It figgered. She hadn't had nothing before worth praying about."

"All right, it figured," Grave Digger conceded. "What did you do then."

"I stayed there, watching all night so she wouldn't get away, but after she turned out the light she didn't get up again. When it got day I had to leave because the people in the windows across the way began watching me suspiciously. I went across the street and watched the door, and when she came out I followed her. When I seen her go into Sweet Prophet's house, I figgered she was giving him the money to keep, so I kissed it goodbye, went to the bar and had some drinks. But after a while I figgered I ought to go back – I was getting tired and hungry by then. And that's when I found her getting ready for the baptism and the picnic. I fell in and went along with her because there wasn't nothing else to do. But when I knowed she hadn't given any money to Sweet Prophet was when she told about her dream –"

"Her dream?" Coffin Ed echoed.

"Yassuh, she jumped up right in the middle of the ceremony and said she had dreamed she was baking three pies and when she took them out the oven they exploded with hundred-dollar bills. I knew then she had played the money row in all three houses and had hit; and I knew she hadn't given the money to Sweet Prophet from the way he licked his chops and his eyes bugged out. I could see it was the first he had heard of it, and I knew she still had the money hidden somewhere. So when she was getting herself baptized, I dropped a little mickey into her bottle of drinking water."

"You had the mickey ready beforehand," Grave Digger said.

"I always carry a mickey," Sugar confessed. "Other folks has their knives and pistols, but I ain't no fighter. And I has to have some kind of way to protect myself. So I just carrys me a little Mickey Finn. But I didn't figger she was going to take the bottle to Sweet Prophet to get it blessed and then start drinking it right away. I figgered she'd drink it while we were having our picnic lunch, and then the other sisters would take her and lay her out somewhere and it would give me a chance to search the house. I didn't have no idea it would cause such a big rumpus. When the people started running and screaming, thinking she'd dropped dead, I beat it before somebody connected me with her and had me held. I had a key to her place what she didn't know about, so I beat it around there and searched it."

"Then you were there before Rufus and the Jew got there?" Grave Digger said.

"It was me that got them there," Sugar confessed. "When I didn't find nothing in the mattress, I remembered that Rufus and the Jew worked this furniture racket, and I made a deal with Rufus to sell the Jew the television set and have him take it away. The way I had it planned was that I'd go get Alberta and bring her home, and when she found the set missing she'd get so scared for her money she'd rush right away to see if it was safe, and I'd find out where it was at. But when I went back to get Alberta, I found out they had taken her away in a hearse and didn't nobody know where she was. So I went back to her place to see if she'd come home but didn't nobody answer. I'd given Rufus my key, so I snuck down the fire escape again and spied through the window. That's when I found out they'd taken all of her furniture."

"You went after Rufus," Grave Digger interjected.

"Yassuh, but not with no knife," Sugar denied. "Rufus claimed he hadn't found the money and that's why he sold all the furniture, but he promised to take another look."

"Then it was Rufus who went to the Jew's warehouse looking for the money," Grave Digger said.

137

"I don't know, boss, I'm just telling you what he said."

"And you went with him," Coffin Ed put in.

"Nawsuh, boss, I didn't even know where it was at."

"The Bronx police figure there were two men there when the Jew was killed," Coffin Ed persisted.

"It sure weren't me," Sugar denied.

"Let him get on," Grave Digger said. "Time is getting short." He asked Sugar, "What were you doing all this time?"

"All I was doing was hanging around outside of Rufus's house watching to see what he would do," Sugar confessed. "He didn't come out until after it got dark – it must have been about nine-thirty – then he got in his car and drove off. I didn't want to be seen hanging around so much in the street, so I went over to Eighth Avenue and hung out in a bar. I was there when I heard the patrol cars passing, and I knew something had happened. When I got back to Manhattan Avenue, I saw the people crowding in the street and the police looking at Rufus's car; and, when I seen the blood on the seat and all over the sidewalk, I knew it was Rufus who'd been stabbed, even before they found him. I didn't want to get caught there, so I moseyed on back to Eighth. And the next thing I knew I saw the cops arresting Alberta, and I figgered they'd be looking for me next so I beat it. I didn't know the Jew had been killed till I went to Alberta's house and the woman there in the window told me. I was scared to stay there; then the next thing I knew Dummy caught up with me on the street and told me the cops was looking for me – as if I didn't know."

"Dummy!" Grave Digger echoed. "What was Dummy doing there?"

"I don't know, boss. I figgered he must have been looking for the money, too."

When he had finished telling the part he had seen Dummy take in the search, he became terrified at the detectives' anger.

"I was just trying to get it back for her," he whined.

"You and Dummy teamed up," Coffin Ed accused.

"Nawsuh, boss, he went his way and I went mine," Sugar denied. "I went back to Alberta's place, got in through the window and searched it again. Then I just went to sleep, boss. I was beat. But somebody else came here whilst I was sleeping, 'cause they left the window open – but I don't know whether it was Dummy or not; I didn't wake up."

"It figures close enough," Grave Digger said. "Only it doesn't leave us much time."

138

"All I'm scared of is somebody might hurt her," Sugar said.

Coffin Ed knocked him off the stool and started to kick him in the face, but Grave Digger restrained him.

"Easy, Ed, he'll keep," he said.

They didn't wait to cross-examine him. They didn't have time. Where before it had been urgent, now it was desperate. They booked him on suspicion and left the station running.

"Dummy first?" Coffin Ed suggested.

"Later," Grave Digger said. "We got to find the woman before they kill her. Let the money go for the time being."

22

Grave Digger turned off the lights before turning the corner and cut off the motor before reaching the entrance. The car coasted to a stop in front of the entrance to the tenement on 118th Street.

"Let's just hope we're right," he said.

They got from the car fast, but with a minimum of sound, and approached the door like grim reapers.

"Pssst!" the big fat black window-watcher called to them.

She looked as though she hadn't left her post. In the shadow she resembled a melted lump of wax.

"If you looking for her, she ain't come back," she said.

Grave Digger felt his heart sink. Coffin Ed grunted as though he had been punched in the stomach. But neither of them hesitated.

The entrance door was closed. Grave Digger gripped the knob and pushed. The door didn't give.

The woman was leaning over the sill, trying to see what he was doing.

"This door is locked," he said.

"Locked!" the woman croaked in amazement. "That door ain't been locked since I lived here, and that's been six years."

"It's locked now. Who has a key?"

Coffin Ed had his pistol out. The long nickel-plated barrel gleamed in the dim light.

"Move over," he said. "I'll blow it open."

"Easy does it," Grave Digger cautioned. "Let's don't risk any noise."

"I got a key," the woman said, groaning as she got from her chair. "But I ain't never used it, and I don't know exactly where it is."

Coffin Ed pushed at the edge of the door. "It ought to break easy enough," he said.

"Take it easy," Grave Digger said tightly. "We don't want to make any graves."

"I found it," the woman called from the window in a stage whisper.

"Give it here," Grave Digger said, leaning over to take it.

"It won't work from the outside," the woman said.

"Then go open it, woman," Grave Digger said savagely. "What's wrong with you?"

They heard her door open softly and padded feet slither across the hall floor. The key was inserted with a slight grating sound, and the rusty bolt creaked as it moved.

They entered the front hall. In the dim light the woman looked about to cave in from exhaustion. The skin of her face had shrunken and turned gray, and lines like spider webs had formed about her eyes, which were as red as live coals.

"I been watching just like you told me," she croaked.

Neither of them answered. With drawn pistols they started up the stairs, taking them three at a time, Grave Digger leading and Coffin Ed at his heels. Their pistols swung in gleaming arcs like the swords of warriors of old.

At the top, they slowed down and moved cautiously. Making as little sound as possible, they bent, their heads together, and listened at the panel of Alberta's door. They did not hear a sound.

Coffin Ed took out his pocket flashlight and held it in his free hand. Grave Digger gripped the knob, tightened it with a slow pull, turned it silently and pushed. The door didn't budge. He took out his own flashlight.

They looked at one another. Grave Digger nodded. They drew back, angled their shoulders and hit the door simultaneously.

The lock broke, and the door was flung back to the wall. They went through the opening side by side and leaped far apart. Their flashlights raked the darkness; their pistols swung in arcs.

The room was empty. The door to the bedroom was closed. In the next flat a man laughed and a woman's voice was heard distinctly through the thin wall: "I tole him his eyes may shine and his teeth may grit . . ." From below, the bass notes from a jazz recording came up through the floor as though someone were hammering on the ceiling with the meaty part of their fist.

They crossed the room on tiptoe and flung open the bedroom door. The drawn shade rustled suddenly in the current of air from the open window, and the muzzles of their pistols leveled in that direction at the height of a man's heart.

The room was empty. They released their breath in a soft sigh and looked at each other again.

"Where do we go from here?" Coffin Ed asked.

Grave Digger nodded toward the kitchen door.

They crossed the room, and Grave Digger opened the door

141

without caution. Their lights focused suddenly on a body lying on the floor.

"Too late," Grave Digger said in a thick cottony voice. "Too late," he repeated bitterly.

"Maybe not," Coffin Ed said.

She lay doubled up on her side on the linoleum floor. She still wore the same uniform in which she had been baptized, but now it was black with dirt. Her hands were tied behind her with a cotton clothesline, which had been run down between her feet and wrapped about her ankles. Her feet had been drawn up to the level of her hands. She was gagged with a yellow bath towel, which was knotted at the back of her head. There was a large red stain on the underside, where blood had soaked into it from the corner of her mouth. Blood, seeping slowly from her greasy matted hair, came from a wound in the top of her head. Her eyes wee closed, and her face looked peaceful. She looked like she was asleep.

Coffin Ed switched on the overhead light, and both detectives holstered their pistols. Grave Digger knelt beside the body and felt for the pulse. Coffin Ed unknotted the gag. She moaned suddenly when the gag was removed and swallowed her tongue. Coffin Ed reached two fingers down her throat and pulled it up, and blood that had collected there poured from her mouth. Grave Digger found a serving spoon in the cupboard drawer and bent the handle to form a hook. Coffin Ed eased his fingers from her mouth while Grave Digger inserted the spoon to hold her tongue in place and hooked the handle over her upper lip.

They found two small burns on each side of her mouth. There were cigarette butts and the stems of burned paper matches on the floor.

"I'll go and call for the ambulance," Coffin Ed said, whispering.

"No need for silence now," Grave Digger said.

He heard Coffin Ed thundering down the stairs as he cut the cotton rope binding her hands and feet and gently straightened out her legs. He found more of the small round burns on the back of her hand. His neck was swollen and corded until the flesh bulged over his collar, and he seemed to have difficulty with his breathing. He lifted her head slightly and inserted a flat pan under her so that it lay level. He didn't turn her over. He didn't touch the wound.

He poked at the cigarette butts with his fingertips. One was the butt of a marijuana cigarette. He didn't bother to pick them up. Finally he got to his feet and looked around, but there was nothing to see.

Coffin Ed returned.

"They're rushing an ambulance from Harlem Hospital," he said, then after a moment added, "Anderson said he'd telephone the Homicide Bureau to see what they wanted done."

"They didn't get anything out of her, so they knocked her in the head," Grave Digger said in a thick, cottony voice.

"They must have had a lookout staked and saw us coming," Coffin Ed surmised.

"I don't dig this business," Grave Digger admitted.

While waiting for the ambulance, they went over the apartment briefly. They saw the signs where Sugar had searched, but nothing to indicate that money had been hidden there. They raised the shade, went out through the bedroom window and climbed the fire escape to the roof. They saw nothing that told them anything. It was easy enough to get down to the street in a dozen places from the flat, adjoining roofs on both 118th and 119th Streets.

"Poking around like this is the long way," Grave Digger said.

"Then it might not lead anywhere," Coffin Ed agreed.

They went back into the kitchen and looked at the woman on the floor.

"Either Slick and his muscle boy, or Dummy alone, or all three together," Coffin Ed said. "Or else somebody we don't know about."

Grave Digger didn't reply.

The sound of a siren came through the night.

"If they were hanging around, they're gone now," Coffin Ed said.

Nothing more was said.

They heard the ambulance draw to a stop down on the street. Steps sounded on the stairs. Two white-clad colored interns came briskly through the front room, one carrying an instrument case. They were followed by a uniformed white driver carrying a rolled-up canvas stretcher.

The interns glanced once at the detectives, then knelt beside the woman and made a quick, cursory examination without opening the instrument case. One pressed the skull gently beside the wound. Alberta moaned.

"Is it bad?" Coffin Ed asked.

"Can't say with concussion," the intern replied without looking up. "Only the X rays will tell. Stretcher," he said to the driver.

The driver unrolled the stretcher and laid it on the floor parallel to the body, and the interns worked the edge underneath her side.

Then, while one intern held her head, the driver and the other intern rolled her over gently on her back onto the stretcher.

"You want something?" the intern asked Coffin Ed.

"Just get her to talk," Grave Digger said in his thick, cottony voice.

"Talking is not good for a concussion case," the intern said.

"Good or not," Grave Digger said brutally.

All three of the ambulance crew looked at him.

The first intern said dispassionately, "All you cops are heartless bastards."

Grave Digger let out his breath. "It's hard to say who's heartless and who isn't," he said. "There's a woman hurt, and there's a killer loose. She can tell us who he is before someone else gets it."

No one answered him.

The driver and one of the interns picked up the stretcher and the other intern, carrying the instrument case, led the way out. The detectives followed.

With the arrival of the ambulance, the tenement had come alive. Tenants crowded into the hallways and peered from open doors.

"Get back into your holes and thank God it isn't you," Coffin Ed said to a group of them.

The window-watcher was waiting in her doorway. Her red eyes peered from a gray face, on which there was a look of consternation.

"I don't see how she could have got in without me seeing her," she said, clutching at Grave Digger's sleeve. "I hardly left the window at all."

He shook her off and passed without replying.

The ambulance was rolling when they got into their car.

"I got a hunch we're just getting started on this thing," Grave Digger said as he unhooked the radio telephone and dialed the precinct station.

"We're going uptown to Five Fifty-five Edgecombe Drive, Slick Jenkins' apartment," he told Lieutenant Anderson. "If anything comes in, you know where to reach us."

"No, wait where you are for the sergeant from Homicide," Anderson directed. "He wants to work this out."

"There isn't time," Grave Digger said.

"Wait anyway," Anderson ordered.

Grave Digger cradled the telephone and started the motor.

"Heartless," he repeated to himself as though it worried him.

23

"Is Slick back?" Grave Digger asked Sam, the doorman.

"Yassuh, boss, he come back about fifteen minutes ago, and I phoned the precinct station like you said," Sam replied.

"Alone?"

"Nawsuh, he got the same boy with him."

"All right, just don't try to play both sides of the street," Grave Digger warned him, and he and Coffin Ed brushed past.

They took the elevator along with two ladies of the night. A rigid silence was maintained. Coffin Ed's grim, acid-burned face was enough to scare the devil out of hell.

The sepia-colored woman with the dyed yellow hair, dressed in the same tight-fitting purple silk Chinese gown, answered their ring again. She opened the door onto the safety chain.

"Yes?"

"We're the police – we're back again," Grave Digger said.

"Slick hasn't come back," she said, beginning to close the door.

"We have a search warrant," Grave Digger said, causing her to hesitate.

"And we don't want to have to shoot open the door," Coffin Ed added.

"May I see it?" she asked resignedly.

Grave Digger took a legal size envelope from his inside coat pocket. It bore the return address of an insurance company. From it he extracted a typewritten letter suggesting that he examine their new life premiums. He unfolded the letter and held it out toward her.

Both detectives had their gazes pinned on her slanting brown eyes. Her eyes looked down in the direction of the letter, but when she reached for it her hand went aside. Grave Digger moved the paper within her grasp. She took it and then instantly returned it.

"I see," she said in a low voice. "Then I will have to let you in."

She had to close the door to unlatch the chain. Both detectives drew their pistols. The chain made a slight rattling sound, followed immediately by the distant sound of a door being opened. A muted voice asked sharply, "Who is it?" They heard her say, "It's two policemen; they have a search warrant," and then the muted voice, lowered to a whisper, saying, "Hold them a minute." There was an almost imperceptible sound of a door closing and a lock clicking shut.

Keys turned inside the entrance door, and bolts moved. She drew the door inward.

"Come in, please."

Holding their pistols in their right hands and their flashlights in their left, they entered a pitch-dark hall.

She closed and locked the door, and turned toward the front of the building.

'Follow me, please."

They tried the doors as they passed. Three opened into darkness, and the fourth was locked. From behind it came the sound of tense whispering, and then a sound like painful retching. Coffin Ed flattened himself against the wall beside the door, while Grave Digger followed the woman through the doorway at the end of the hall into the front sitting room. It was lit by a floor lamp and a table lamp, and through the three front windows the terraced lights of the Bronx were visible.

From behind the other door to the locked room Grave Digger heard a sharp gasp and the muffled sound of scuffling. Then a key was being turned.

The thick, enraged voice of an imbecile shouted, *"He's gittin' away!"*

Grave Digger was already moving toward the closed door, but the woman blocked the way. He reached out to push her aside, but the motion was arrested by the sight of Dummy coming through the opened door. Blood was coming from his mouth, and he was mewling like a cat.

"He's hurt my cat!" the woman cried hysterically.

Grave Digger felt the hair rise on his head.

The heavy thunder of two shots from an automatic gun crashed, one after another. They were followed almost simultaneously by the hard, deafening impact of Coffin Ed's .38 as he shot through the lock in the hall door.

A big broad-shouldered man wearing cowboy boots and a beaver hat staggered after Dummy through the open door. Dummy took four steps into the room and fell face downward on the carpet. The big man fell like a log right behind him. His hat flew off, and his face smashed into the sole of Dummy's canvas sneaker.

146

Then from the room came the low grating sound of Coffin Ed's voice, saying, "Drop it," sounding as dangerous as a rattlesnake's rattle.

Grave Digger leaped over the big man's body, knocking the woman to her knees, and went into the room with his pistol ready.

The room was a bedroom, with twin beds covered with green chenille spreads. Beyond the second bed Slick stood motionless, looking straight ahead. He wore a pink flannel smoking jacket with a blue velvet collar, and in the soft light from the single bed table lamp his thin, ascetic face was expressionless. The blued steel .38 caliber automatic lay on the bedspread in front of him.

Coffin Ed stood just inside the hall door with its shattered lock. His .38 caliber revolver hung motionless at his side. From the muzzle of its long nickel-plated barrel came a lingering wisp of smoke, adding to the tingling smell of cordite in the room.

Grave Digger lowered his pistol and let out his breath.

"All right, bring him in here," he said, turning to re-enter the sitting room.

The woman was on her hands and knees, rocking from side to side.

Dummy lay on his belly with his arms spread out and his face turned to one side. The handle of the knife Susie had been sharpening on his boot earlier in the day protruded from the center of his back, between the shoulder blades. He was breathing in soft shallow gasps, and shaking his head almost imperceptibly. His brown eyes peered from beneath the lumps of scar tissue with the pleading look of a sick dog.

"Don't worry, I won't pull out the knife," Grave Digger assured him, and gave his attention to the other man.

Susie had two bullet holes in the back of his heavy tweed coat, from one of which the heavy pumping of blood was beginning to ebb. He had the absolutely motionless, relaxed, gone-for-good look of the brand-new dead.

"Straight through the ticker," Grave Digger muttered.

He stood aside as Coffin Ed ushered Slick into the room.

Without looking at the body, Slick stepped over it. He stepped past the woman without looking at her either, and stood with his hands raised shoulder high. He didn't move while Coffin Ed frisked him.

"He killed my cat," the woman said suddenly, and began to cry hysterically.

"Jesus Christ!" Grave Digger said.

Holstering his gun, he put his hands beneath the woman's arms and lifted her gently to her feet.

"Your cat is all right," he said. "This man called Dummy was stabbed, and your husband shot his partner in the back."

She seemed reassured. He helped her to the chaise longue and laid her down. Then he turned and looked at Slick.

"Now I know why they call you Slick," he said.

Slick didn't answer.

Grave Digger found a telephone on a table near the door. He telephoned Harlem Hospital for an ambulance and then contacted Lieutenant Anderson at the Precinct Station.

"Hold everything," Anderson ordered. "Sergeant Frick from the Homicide Bureau is on his way up there now."

"Right," Grave Digger said.

"I don't know anything about these people," Slick said. "They've been trying to proposition me into helping them rob some woman, but I nixed them off. They came here tonight to try again. When you people came, each one accused the other of stooling. I had to shoot the big guy, Susie, to keep him from killing the little dummy."

The detectives stared at him. Neither bothered to answer.

After a moment Slick added sardonically, "I got a soft heart."

Grave Digger slapped him with the open palm of his right hand with such force that he spun three feet, straight into Coffin Ed's short right to his belly. They beat him until the doorbell rang, one slapping and the other punching – not hard enough to bruise, just hard enough to hurt.

The room was beginning to empty. For a time it had been crowded.

The ambulance had come and taken Dummy.

An assistant Medical Examiner had arrived and examined the body. He had written on the tag that was later tied to the right big toe:

NAME: *Susie Green*
AGE: *apprx. 26*
NATIONALITY: *colored*
ADDRESS: *unknown*
DIED: *murdered by two gunshot wounds penetrating the back of the thorax, one penetrating the heart*

The body had begun its lonely journey to the morgue.

Sergeant Frick had arrived with two assistant detectives. They remained.

A table had been dragged to the center of the floor, and Sergeant Frick sat behind it. One of the detectives sat beside him with a pad and stylo to take down the preliminary statements.

"I'll talk to the woman first and get her out of the way," Frick said.

"I had better tell you, she's blind," Grave Digger said.

The woman pulled her knees beneath her and hunched forward on the chaise longue.

"I'm blind, but I can hear," she said.

The five policemen stared at her with varying emotions.

Slick, sprawled in an armchair against the inner wall, said menacingly, "Just keep your mouth shut, bitch."

His face was swollen, as though he had run into a nest of hornets, and his discolored eyes were almost shut.

Coffin Ed reached over and slapped him across the mouth. Slick didn't move.

"No more of that," Sergeant Frick said sharply.

Grave Digger leaned against the wall, looking into the distance.

"I want to make a statement," the woman said in a tired, dead voice. "Slick killed the Jew."

Grave Digger pushed from the wall, and his body tensed. The other four policemen froze.

Slick sat forward in his chair. "Bitch, if you try to frame me, I'll kill you, if it takes all my life to do it," he threatened in a deadly voice.

"Take him out," Frick said.

Grave Digger reached down, clamped Slick back of the neck and yanked him to his feet. Coffin Ed took him by the arm.

"Let Haines take him – I want you two here," Frick said.

The second white detective from the Homicide Bureau hand-cuffed Slick's hands behind him and marched him down the hall toward the kitchen.

"Go on," Frick told the woman.

"Slick knew that a woman named Alberta Wright hit the numbers for thirty-six thousand dollars," the woman said.

The detective scratched rapidly on his pad.

"He propositioned Susie to rob her on a half-and-half basis," she went on. "He told Susie where she lived and gave him the setup. Susie went down to rob her, but he didn't get a chance. Her man was hanging around outside her window all night. But Susie got a chance to see her hide the money in her mattress before he was chased away. When he got back on Sunday and looked through the window, he saw Rufus there. He went down the street to wait for Rufus to leave, but the Jew came with his moving van and started taking away all of her furniture. So he stole the mattress from the van. But the money wasn't in the mattress.

"He came here Sunday afternoon and told Slick what had happened. Slick thought that either Rufus or the Jew had found the money; he didn't know which. He and Susie left the house and were gone for about an hour. I heard them talking when they came back. They had found out where Rufus lived, but they weren't sure he had found the money, and they didn't know where the Jew had taken the furniture. Slick decided he'd watch Rufus. He told Susie to wait here for a telephone call in case he would need him. He telephoned here Sunday night, sometime between ten-thirty and eleven o'clock. When I heard the phone ring I went to the kitchen and listened in on the extension.

"Slick told Susie that the Jew had searched the furniture and had found the money. He said he had followed Rufus to the Jew's place in the Bronx and had seen the Jew find the money. He said he had trapped the Jew and killed him; he didn't say how he had done it; but he said the Jew had given the money to Rufus and that Rufus had got away. Susie asked him how he had let Rufus get away, and he said Rufus had stabbed him in the shoulder. He told Susie to go to Rufus's place on Manhattan Avenue and get the money from him before he could get into his house and hide it.

"When Slick came home he gave me the clothes he was wearing and told me to get rid of them. Then he went into the bathroom, and bandaged his shoulder and had me fix him three pipes of opium. Before he went to sleep, he told me to wake him up when Susie called. Susie didn't call at all that night, and it was morning when Slick woke up. He thought that Susie had double-crossed him. He had dressed and had started out to look for Susie when Susie came here. Susie told him he had got the money from Rufus, but it was only Confederate money. Slick didn't believe him.

"Susie had some plan of using the money for a confidence game to beat Sweet Prophet, and Slick agreed. They went out together and came back a couple of hours later with the money they had made. But Slick wasn't satisfied; he still thought Susie was trying to trick him. They left again when Slick went to work – he was a payoff man for the Tia Juana house – and when they came back they brought Dummy. There was a fight, and Slick drew his pistol on Dummy.

150

"Later on Slick called up a bail-bondsman and had him go Alberta Wright's bail. When the bondsman phoned around eight o'clock to say that Alberta Wright was out, they left the house. They got back a few minutes before the policemen arrived.

She stopped talking suddenly and waited for someone else to speak.

Frick looked from Grave Digger to Coffin Ed.

"Do you believe it?" he asked them.

The detectives exchanged looks.

"I believe it," Grave Digger said. "It figures all around."

"It's just her word," Frick said. "She hasn't offered any substantiating evidence."

"You'll find the clothes he was wearing in my overnight case in the bedroom clothes closet," she said. "There's a pocketbook in one of the pockets that might mean something. And you ought to be able to find some kind of evidence in his car – maybe he stepped in some blood or something."

"Get the bag," Frick said, but Coffin Ed had already moved.

It contained the suit, with the blood splotch around a small cut on the left shoulder, just as she had said. In the inside coat pocket was an old worn billfold with half a dozen cellophane card holders containing licenses and identifications made out to Abraham Finkelstein.

"This might do it," Frick said. "But, as his wife, she won't be allowed to testify against him, and we will need her statement to make it stick."

"I'm not his wife," she said in that tired, dead voice. "I'm just a woman he blinded, beating me with his fists."

During the embarrassed silence that followed, no one looked at anybody else.

"Did you believe her?" Coffin Ed asked as they drove leisurely down Seventh Avenue, returning to the station to write up their report.

"Hell, no," Grave Digger said with an almost inaudible chuckle.

"It's more likely that Rufus killed the Jew."

"Sure it was Rufus."

"And it was Susie who attacked Rufus, trying to get the money," Coffin Ed surmised.

"That's the way I have it figured too," Grave Digger agreed. "Susie had Slick's car and followed Rufus to the Bronx then beat him back home and killed him."

151

"But she'll make it stick," Coffin Ed said.

"Yeah, she'll pay him off," Grave Digger confirmed.

Dummy never reported the tan jumper with the bloodstained shoulder he had found in Susie's hotel room, and the police never discovered it. It stayed like the woman said.

24

For six days Alberta lay in bed in a ward with nine other women. Her head was swathed in bandages; her flat, pretty, brown-skinned face was sullen.

Police came to see her; friends came to see her; Sugar Stonewall came to see her; Dummy came in a wheel chair from another ward to see her. She did not speak a single word to anyone. She lay there with her mouth shut tight and wouldn't even say hello.

During that time sympathetic attendants washed her uniform and cleaned her once-white shoes.

On the seventh day, another Monday, she ate her breakfast in dead silence, as usual.

Then the nurse brought her clothes and gave her permission to get up and walk about the ward.

She got dressed in her clean white uniform and wrapped her pink-checked hand towel about the bandages on her head. She walked up and down the ward two or three times, then went out into the corridor. No one stopped her; no one seemed to notice her.

As though by instinct, she went downstairs to the kitchen. It was a big kitchen with a lot of people working in it, all of them clad in white uniforms. The head cook thought she was a new helper and put her to work peeling potatoes.

She got a long sharp paring knife and sat down on a wooden stool before a five-gallon can of spuds and went to work. By ten-thirty o'clock she had finished with that can. She quit, stuck the paring knife into the pocket of her uniform, got up and walked out.

Instinctively, she found the service exit. The guard on duty gave her scarcely a glance as she passed on her way out of the building; to him she looked like any number of hospital workers.

It was not far down Lenox Avenue to 116th Street. No one on the street paid her the slightest attention.

She turned over on 116th Street to the Temple of Wonderful Prayer and went upstairs to Sweet Prophet's reception room.

Elder Jones congratulated her on being well again, and told her to wait and he would see if Sweet Prophet could give her an audience.

Sweet Prophet sat behind his desk, clad in the same shining garments he had worn the previous Monday, when she had last seen him. Evidently it was his Monday outfit.

When Elder Jones informed him that Alberta Wright wished to see him, he exclaimed, "That woman again! My God, she's got more lives than a cat!"

But he was prevailed upon to give her an audience.

He looked more than ever like the rising sun as she came into the room. She walked toward his desk with her hands in her pockets. The secretary, standing behind the Prophet, looked at her compassionately.

Sweet Prophet was searching in his pocket for the crumb he expected her to buy. He looked up with a patient expression and said, "My child, what's troubling you this time?"

She leaned one hand on the desk, whipped the paring knife out of her pocket with the other hand and plunged it into the left side of his chest with such force that only the handle protruded.

He gasped and dropped forward over the desk like a stone.

Twenty minutes later, it was announced to the people crowded in the street that word had come from Harlem Hospital that he would live.

The blade had penetrated the left pleura, but had missed the aorta by a hair's breadth.

By that time Alberta was in the booking room of the Harlem Precinct Station, surrounded by bug-eyed cops.

Finally Sergeant Ratigan, the day man from the Homicide Bureau, who had been on the case from the beginning, arrived. He had brought along his own stenographer, and he took over the precinct captain's office for the interrogation. The captain sat in, as did several precinct detectives.

Alberta sat in a straight-backed chair, looking composed and resigned as she faced the battery of officers behind the desk.

"Why did you do it, Alberta?" Ratigan asked in what he mistakenly thought was a kindly tone of voice.

"He stole my money," Alberta replied in the whining Southern voice she employed when talking to white people.

Ratigan's eyes popped in amazement, but he controlled his voice.

"How did he steal your money?" he asked, as though reasoning with a child.

"I gave it to him," she said.

"Oh," Ratigan said. "But that doesn't mean he stole it."

"Nawsuh, but he didn't give it back."

154

"All right, let's get this straight," Ratigan said. "You gave him the money, and he didn't give it back. Did you ask him for it?"

"Nawsuh. I forgot I gave it to him."

Slowly, and at first unnoticeably, she began to cry.

"All right," Ratigan said. "Don't get upset. Take your time and tell me just what happened."

She swallowed. "I went to him Sunday morning to pay for to get baptized," she said, "and I told him I needed to get religion because I had won all that money on the numbers."

"It was thirty-six thousand, wasn't it?" Ratigan asked.

"Yassuh, but I didn't have but twenty-nine thousand, four hundred left," she said.

"Yes, go on," Ratigan prompted.

Everyone in the room was staring at her unblinkingly, their mouths half open as though their breathing were suspended.

"He told me to look him straight in the eye," she said. "I kept looking him in the eyes until my head seemed to get empty of everything but just his eyes. Then he said, 'You will do exactly as I say.' And I said, 'Yes, Sweet Prophet.' He said, 'Go back to your house and get all the money from where it is hidden and bring it to me.' I said, 'Yes Sweet Prophet.'

"And I went and got the money and brought it back and gave it to him. He took it and put it away, and then he looked me in the eye again and said, 'You will forget everything you have done since you came into this room.' And I said, 'Yes Sweet Prophet.'

"And the next thing I knew I was sitting there talking to him about getting baptized, and I had forgotten everything else. I had no idea where my money had gone until I came to in the hospital after I had got knocked on the head. Then I remembered everything. He knowed I was looking for my money, and he wouldn't give it back."

She started crying out loud. Her big-boned body was racked by uncontrollable paroxysms.

The hard-boiled cops stared at her in awe.

"He thought I didn't know anything about hypnotism," she wailed. "He thought I was just a big simple fool. He didn't have to go and hypnotize me and take my money and then try to keep it," she blubbered. "I would have given it all to him if he had just come right out and asked for it."

Ratigan stared at her in speechless amazement. "You mean you would have given that charlatan all of that huge sum of money that you won if he had asked for it? Good God, woman, why?"

"Because I believed in him," she said, crying almost hysterically now. "That's why. If you is a black woman like me, you got to believe in something."

Sergeant Ratigan had intended to ask her, during the course of the interrogation, why she had gone with Slick and Susie up to her empty flat where they had tortured her and struck her in the head, but now he didn't have the heart.

"The chances are the court is going to let you off if the prophet pulls through, and it looks as though he will," Ratigan said. "Now don't you go and stab your man Sugar, next, because you might kill him, and that will be serious."

She looked up puzzled. "What's he done?"

Ratigan was flustered. "Oh, I thought you knew that he was trying to steal your money, too."

A tiny smile peeped through her tears. "Oh, I ain't mad at him for that," she said. "He was just doing what comes natural."

Ratigan called it a finish. A matron came and locked her up until the wagon came to take her downtown again for arraignment next morning.

No sooner had the key turned in the lock than she was singing:

"I'm blue
But I wont be blue always
'Cause the sun's going to shine in my back door
Some day."

Some days later, when Sweet Prophet was asked by members of the colored press why he had taken her money, he replied,

"I needed it. It takes a lot of money to be a prophet these days. It's the high cost of living."

Allison & Busby American Crime Series

CHESTER HIMES

"A crime writer of Chandlerian subtlety, though in a vein of sheer toughness very much his own" – *The Times*

"The books have lasting value – as thrillers, as streetwise documentries, as chapters of black writing at its ribald and unaffected best. They are simply – or rather, not so simply, terrific" – *The Sunday Times*

The Heat's On

The Heat's On is one of the fastest, funniest and hardest hitting thrillers Chester Himes ever wrote. From the start nothing goes right for ace black detectives, Coffin Ed Johnson and Grave Digger Jones. Try as they might, they always seem to be one hot step behind the cause of all the mayhem – three million dollars worth of heroin and a simple albino called Pinky.

Blind Man with a Pistol

This was the last Harlem novel Chester Himes wrote. In it Coffin Ed Johnson and Grave Digger Jones are trying as ever to keep the peace, their nickel-plated ·38s very much in evidence. But this time they find themselves pursuing two completely different cases through a maze of knifings, beatings, and street riots. The risk is always that the disappearing killer and the answer to a grim problem will collide and tear Harlem apart at its bursting seams.

Also available as Allison & Busby paperbacks:

Cotton Comes to Harlem
The Crazy Kill
A Rage in Harlem
The Real Cool Killers

Allison & Busby American Crime Series

RICHARD STARK

"Nobody tops Stark in his objective portrayals of a world of total amorility" – *New York Times*

"A true existentialist . . . Parker conducts his business between the twin worlds of organised crime and disorganised society" – *City Limits*

Point Blank

Double-crossed, shot and left for dead in a burning house by his wife and one-time partner, Parker is out for revenge. He's also out for his share of the take, and if that means taking on the Outfit, Parker doesn't care. He's owed $45,000 and he's going to get it.

The Man with the Getaway Face

Outwitting the Syndicate means Parker must buy a new face. But once the bandages are off, keeping the new identity secret becomes a full-time occupation.

The Jugger

Jo Sheer was Parker's contract man. Now he's dead. But before he died he talked, and what he knew could nail Parker to the wall with a hundred nails.

The Black Ice Score

Stealing the African's diamonds back from the museum in the heart of New York appeals to the arch-pro in Parker, but the oppisition's clumsy double-cross brings out his mean streak.

The Green Eagle Score

Parker plans to steal the entire payroll from a US Air Force base up near the Canadian border. The heist goes like a dream, but the split turns sour.

Allison & Busby American Crime Series

STEPHEN DOBYNS

"More than just a hardboiled Dick Francis, Dobyns writes real people" – *Time Out*

"Saratoga is a beguiling setting . . . It's non-stop reading, and Dobyns gets it right" – Richard Ford

"His writing is honest, tough-minded and as uncompromising as his unforgettable hero" – Lawrence Block, *Washington Post*

Sartoga Headhunter

Ex-cop Charlie Bradshaw's new career as a private detective is progressing so quietly his successful cousins try to persuade him he should take a job as a milkman. But then one night Jimmy McClatchy turns up on his doorstep looking for a place to hide. And when Jimmy – a jockey who's turned States' Evidence in a Federal trial – winds up dead at Charlie's table, the reluctant detective's new career begins in earnest.

Saratoga Swimmer

Shortly after leaving the Saratoga police department, Charlie Bradshaw is hired as head security guard at Lew Ackerman's extensive racing stables. Ackerman has quickly become a friend of Charlie's as well as being his boss. Then Ackerman is bloodily murdered in the town's swimming-pool and Charlie makes it his final act of friendship to find out why.

Allison & Busby American Crime Series

MAX BYRD

"Max Byrd is in the first division of American Crime writing" –
The Times

"All that we remember as best from Hammett, Chandler and
Macdonald" – *New Republic*

Finders Weepers

It all started when Leo Matz hired Mike Haller to find a prostitute
who'd been left $800,000. Within hours of taking the case Haller is
framed for a shooting he didn't do and his PI licence has been revoked.
But whoever fixed the frame-up has misjudged Haller badly, and that
will cost him and a lot of other people dear.

California Thriller

When a leading San Fransisco journalist vanishes into the thin air of the
Sacramento valley, Haller is the man the editor sends for. The trouble is
someone else wants the journalist to stay lost – preferably for ever.